"If that bullet had been half an inch closer…" The man suddenly bowed his head and winced.

Skylar was taken aback by his reaction. "Joe? What's wrong? I'm okay."

"Right." He lifted his head and his jaw pulsed with tension. "You always were able to take care of yourself."

He'd learned exactly what she'd hoped to teach him about her. Regrettably.

Skylar lifted her chin bravely. "Still can take care of myself."

"Being shot at is no way to go about it, Skylar. If anything would have happened to you…" He winced again and looked aside, toward the firepit.

Skylar found herself leaning forward in hopes of him finishing that sentence.

WITNESS IN THE WOODS

USA TODAY Bestselling Author

MICHELE HAUF

Recycling programs
for this product may
not exist in your area.

ISBN-13: 978-1-335-60474-3

Witness in the Woods

Copyright © 2019 by Michele Hauf

This edition published by arrangement with Harlequin Books S.A.

For questions and comments about the quality of this book, please contact us at CustomerService@Harlequin.com.

® and TM are trademarks of Harlequin Enterprises Limited or its corporate affiliates. Trademarks indicated with ® are registered in the United States Patent and Trademark Office, the Canadian Intellectual Property Office and in other countries.

Printed in U.S.A.

Michele Hauf is a *USA TODAY* bestselling author who has been writing romance, action-adventure and fantasy stories for more than twenty years. France, musketeers, vampires and faeries usually feature in her stories. And if Michele followed the adage "write what you know," all her stories would have snow in them. Fortunately, she steps beyond her comfort zone and writes about countries and creatures she has never seen. Find her on Facebook, Twitter and at michelehauf.com.

Books by Michele Hauf

Harlequin Intrigue

Storm Warning
Witness in the Woods

Harlequin Nocturne

The Witch's Quest
The Witch and the Werewolf
An American Witch in Paris
The Billionaire Werewolf's Princess
Tempting the Dark
This Strange Witchery

The Saint-Pierre Series

The Dark's Mistress
Ghost Wolf
Moonlight and Diamonds
The Vampire's Fall
Enchanted by the Wolf

In the Company of Vampires

Beautiful Danger
The Vampire Hunter
Beyond the Moon

Visit the Author Profile page at Harlequin.com.

CAST OF CHARACTERS

Joseph Cash—A conservation officer with the Minnesota Department of Natural Resources. Joe's investigation into a local poaching ring will rip a trusted friend from his life and bring him back to the woman he has always desired.

Skylar Davis—A small-animal veterinarian who rehabs rescue animals. Her only dream is to build a sanctuary for all the animals who need help. But will her family allow that to happen?

Max Owen—The elderly Chippewa naturalist who took Joseph under his wing when he was a child and became his lifelong mentor, teaching him to respect the wild.

Stella—The timber wolf Skylar rescued as a pup; lost a leg to a snare trap.

Cole Pruitt—Skylar's ex-fiancé has a new job, a new address and a big secret.

Malcolm Davis—Skylar's uncle, who lives on the property bordering her land and owns Davis Trucking. He's known for poaching, and getting away with it, but what else is he doing to evade the law?

Dorothy Davis—Skylar's long-lost mother. The things she doesn't know could change Skylar's life forever.

Chapter One

Joseph Cash raced toward the admittance doors of St. Luke's emergency room. He'd driven furiously from Lake Seraphim the moment he'd heard the dispatcher's voice announce that an elderly Indian man near death had been found crawling at the edge of County Road 7. A young couple had spotted him, pulled over and called the police.

Joe had responded to Dispatch and asked if he could take the call. She'd reported back that an ambulance was already at the scene and the man was being transferred to Duluth. The patient was seizing, and the initial report had been grim. They couldn't know if he'd arrive alive or dead.

The description the dispatcher had given Joe could have been that of any elderly Native American. Sun-browned skin, long dark hair threaded with gray and pulled into a ponytail. Estimated age around eighty.

But Joe instinctually knew who the man was. His heart had dropped when he'd heard the location where the man had been found climbing up out of the ditch on all fours. That was the one place Max Owen had used to rendezvous with Joe when he brought him provisions, because from there it was a straight two-mile hike through the thick Boundary Waters to where he'd camped every summer for twenty years in a little tent at the edge of a small lake.

Joe hadn't seen Max since June, two months earlier. He'd looked well, though his dry cough had grown more pronounced over the past year. Max had attributed it to the bad habit of smoking when he'd been a teenager. If anything happened to end that old man before Joe could see him—no, he mustn't think like that.

Now he entered the too-bright, fluorescent-lit hallway of the ER intake area. Three people queued before the admissions desk, waiting to be assessed for triage. Normally, Joe would respectfully wait his turn, as he had occasion to check in on patients he'd brought here himself while on duty as a conservation officer with the Minnesota Department of Natural Resources.

Fingers curling impatiently in and out of his fists, he stepped from foot to foot. He couldn't wait. If the emergency crew hadn't been certain about Max's condition…

"The Native American man who was brought in," he said over the head of a stooped elderly woman at the front of the line.

The male nurse behind the bulletproof glass glanced up and, at the sight of Joe, smiled. Though weariness etched the nurse's brow, his eyes glinted. "Hey, handsome, who you looking for?"

"An old man was found on County Road 7 about forty-five minutes ago. Dispatch says they brought him here." He wore the conservation officer's green jacket over his matching forest-green cotton shirt, so he had the official gear to grant him authority. But it probably wouldn't matter, Joe decided, as the nurse winked at him.

"Please, I don't mean to interrupt, ma'am." Joe flashed a smile at the old woman who was giving him the stink eye. "I think I know him. I can provide identification. He's eighty-two, Native American..." Joe thought about it less than a moment, then clasped his fingers at his neck. "And he always wore an eagle talon on a leather choker at his neck."

The nurse nodded. "We got your guy." He glanced at the computer screen before him and then muttered, "Oh."

That single utterance dropped Joe's heart to his gut. Because he knew. The nurse didn't need to say anything more.

Wincing through the sudden rise of sadness that welled in his chest, Joe nodded toward the doors that led to the treatment rooms. The nurse touched the security button, which released the lock on the doors, and Joe dashed through, calling back a mumbled thanks.

He hadn't bothered to ask for a room number. There were only two rooms designated for those bodies that awaited the coroner's visit. He knew that from previous visits. Walking swiftly down the hallway, he beat a fist into his palm as he neared the first room. The walls were floor-to-ceiling windows. All the curtains had been pulled, and no light behind them shone out.

"Officer?" A short blonde nurse in maroon scrubs appeared by his side and looked up at him. She smelled like pink bubblegum.

"I heard the dispatch call on the old man," Joe said. "I may be able to identify him."

"Excellent. We thought he was a John Doe. I'll just need your badge and name for our records. Why don't you step inside the room and take a look to confirm your guess while I grab some forms?"

"Is he…? When did he—?"

"He was DOA. Dr. Preston called it ten minutes ago. Presented as ingestion of a poisonous substance, but we're waiting for the coroner to do a thorough workup. I'll be right back!"

She was too cheery, but then Joe had learned that the ER sported all ranges of personalities, and it was those who exuded cheer who survived longest the grueling emotional toll such work forced upon them. Either that, or she was faking it to get through yet another endless shift.

He opened the sliding door, which glided too quietly, and stepped inside the room. Though the body on the bed was covered from head to toe with a white sheet, he just knew. The ten-year-old boy inside him shook his head and sucked in his lower lip. Not fair. Why Max?

Carefully, Joe tugged back the sheet from the head. Recognition seized his heart. He caught a gasp at the back of his throat.

"Oh, Max." Joe swore softly and gripped the steel bed rail. The man had been so kind to him over the years. He was literally the reason Joe currently worked for the DNR.

Poison? But how? It made no sense.

The sudden arrival of the nurse at his side startled him. She moved like a mouse, fast and stealthily.

"Sorry." She handed him a clipboard and then turned on a low light over the bed. "Just need your signature. Do you recognize the deceased?"

"I do." Joe scribbled his name and badge number on the standard form and handed it back to her. "His name is Maximilien Owen and he's Chippewa. The Fond du Lac band. Doesn't live on the Fond du Lac reservation, though. Hasn't associated closely with his tribe for decades. Eighty-two years old. Has never seen a doctor a day in his life. I thought he was healthy, though he'd had a dry cough of late. Are you sure it was poison?"

"That was the initial assessment. You know these Native Americans have herbs and plants they use for rituals and whatnot. Probably ate the wrong plant or something. It's very sad," she added.

Joe lifted a brow. She had no idea.

"Max would never eat the wrong plant," Joe insisted. "He lived off the land his entire life. He knew the Boundary Waters like no one else. His dad used to be a tracker in the Vietnam War, and he taught Max everything he knew."

"Oh, that's touching."

She wasn't in the mood to hear the old man's life story, and Joe wasn't going to gift her with Max's wonderful tale. He pegged her cheery attitude as a false front.

"I'm going to stick around for the coroner," he said. "I want an autopsy."

The nurse's jaw dropped. "Do you…know his family? We don't usually…"

"He didn't have family. I'll pay for the autopsy. This is important."

Joe wasn't about to let the old man be filed away as an accidental poisoning. That was not Max. At all. Something wasn't right. And Joe would not rest until it was confirmed that Max's death had been natural—or not.

Two weeks later…

BURNING CEDARWOOD SWEETENED the air better than any fancy department store perfume Skylar Davis had ever smelled. Pine and elm kindling crackled in the bonfire before her. A refreshingly cool August breeze swept in from the lake not thirty yards away and caressed her shoulders. She breathed in, closing her eyes, and hugged the heavy white satin wedding dress against her chest.

It was time to do this.

Beside her on the grass, alert and curious, sat Stella, the three-year-old timber wolf she'd rescued as a pup. Skylar could sense the wolf's positive, gentle presence. The wolf was there for her. No matter what.

She opened her eyes and then dropped the wedding dress onto the fire. Smoke coiled. Sparks snapped. Stella sounded an are-you-sure-about-this yip.

"Has to be done, Stella. I can't move forward any other way."

Using a long, charred oak stick peeled clean of bark—her father's fire-poking stick—she nudged the lacy neckline of the dress deeper into the flames. The tiny pearls glowed, then blackened, and the lace quickly melted. The frothy concoction, woven with hopes and dreams—and a whole lot of reckless abandon—meant little to her now.

Stepping back to stand beside Stella, Skylar planted the tip of the fire-poking stick in the ground near her boot and nodded. She should have done this two months earlier—that Saturday afternoon when she'd found herself marching into the county courthouse with hell in her eyes and fury in her heart. An unexpected conversation with her uncle an hour earlier had poked through her heart and left it ragged.

Her world had tilted off balance that day. The man she'd thought she was ready to share the rest of her life with had a secret life that he'd attempted to keep from her. She'd had her suspicions about Cole Pruitt, which was why she had been the one to approach Uncle Malcolm in the flower shop parking lot that morning she had intended to say *I do*. Normally she'd find a way to walk a wide circle around the family member who had done nothing but serve her and her father heartache over the years. But she'd had to know. And Malcolm had been just evasive enough for her to press—until he'd spilled the truth about Cole.

Since then, life had been strangely precarious. Not only had she ditched a fiancé, but her uncle had been keeping a close eye on her, as well. Hounding her about the parcel of land he wanted her to sell to him. And so close to making threats, but not quite. Still, she was

constantly looking over her shoulder for something—
danger, or…a rescuer?

Hell, she was a strong, capable woman who could
take care of herself. She didn't need rescuing.

Maybe.

"Stella, I—"

Something stung Skylar's ear. It felt like a mosquito,
but immediately following that sudden burn, she saw
wood split out, and a small hole appeared through the
old hitching post three feet to her right.

"What the—?"

Clamping a hand over her ear and instinctively ducking, Skylar let out a gasp as another hole suddenly
drilled into the post.

Stella jumped to all fours, alert and whining in a low
and warning tone. The wolf scanned the woods that surrounded their circle of a backyard. Cutting the circle
off on the bottom was the rocky lakeshore. A cleared
swath in the thick birch and maple woods opened to
the lake, where Skylar saw no boat cruising by. Was
someone in the woods?

She opened her hand before her. Blood smeared one
of her fingers. What had just happened?

The holes in the post answered that question. And
set Skylar's heartbeats to a faster pace.

"Stella, stay here." Still in a squat, Skylar patted her
thigh. The wolf crept to her side and Skylar ran her fingers through her soft summer coat. "Someone just shot
at me," she whispered.

And, unfortunately, that was no surprise.

Chapter Two

Finishing off a ham-and-pickle sandwich he'd packed for a late lunch, Joe Cash sat in his county-issue four-by-four pickup truck outside the public access turnoff to Lake Vaillant. He'd just come off the water after a long day patrolling, which involved checking that fishermen had current licenses, guiding a few lost tourists in the right direction and issuing a warning to a group of teens who had been trying to dive for "buried treasure." The depths of the lake were littered with fishing line, lost hooks and decades of rusting boat parts. Only the beach on the east shore had been marked for safe swimming.

All in a day's work. A man couldn't ask for a better job. Conservation officer for the Minnesota Department of Natural Resources was a title that fit Joe to a tee. Ninety percent of the time, his office featured open air, lakes, trees, snow and/or sun. Joe's job was to keep the public safe, but also to protect and guard the wildlife that flourished in this county set in the Superior Forest. Not a day passed that he didn't get to wander through tall grasses, spot a blue heron or, if he was lucky, spy on a timber wolf from a local pack.

He smiled widely and tilted back the steel canteen of lukewarm water for a few swallows. This job was what made him wake with a smile and dash out to work every morning. Nothing could give him more satisfaction. Except, that is, when he finally nailed the parties responsible for the rampant poaching in the area. Someone, or many someones, had been poaching deer, beaver, cougar, turkey and the animal most precious to Joe's soul, the gray wolf. But tops on the list was the bald eagle. Taking down the other animals without a proper license was considered a gross misdemeanor. Taking down a bald eagle was a federal offense. And recently he'd begun to wonder if the poachers were using something beyond the usual snare or steel trap. Like death by poisoning.

The autopsy on Max Owen had shown he'd been poisoned by strychnine. He hadn't consumed it orally, but rather, it had permeated his skin and entered his bloodstream. And even more surprising than the poison? His lungs had been riddled with cancer. That discovery had troubled Joe greatly. If he had known what was growing in Max, he would have taken him to a doctor long ago. The poison had killed him, but it was apparent the cancer would have been terminal. The coroner had ruled his death accidental. There had been no evidence of foul play. Max must have handled the poison improperly, it was determined.

Joe knew the old man was not stupid. He didn't handle poison. Strychnine was rarely used, and if so, only by farmers for weeds and crops. Max had immense respect for wildlife and would never use or put something into the environment that could cause harm.

After saying goodbye to his mentor in the ER that night, Joe had gone directly to the site where Max set up his campsite from April to October. It had been past midnight, but Joe had tromped through the woods, confident in his destination. Yet when he'd arrived at camp, he had been too emotionally overwhelmed to do a proper evidence search. Instead, he'd sat against the oak tree where Max had always crossed his legs and showered wisdom on Joe. He had cried, then fallen asleep. In the morning, Joe had pulled on latex gloves and gathered evidence. There hadn't been clear signs of unwelcome entry to the site, no containers that might have held the poison, but Joe had gathered all the stored food and the hunting knife Max used and taken it in to Forensics. The forensic specialist had reported all those items were clean. Whatever Max had touched was still out there, had been tucked somewhere away from the campsite or had been thrown.

And while the county had seemed to want to brush it off—the old man was dead and he hadn't had any family—the tribe had seen to the burial of his body.

Joe had insisted he be allowed to continue with the investigation. The tribal police had given him permission, as they were not pursuing the death, having accepted the accidental poison ruling as final.

He might not have been family by blood, but Max was true family to Joe. He'd been there for Joe when he was a kid, and had literally saved his life. And he had been the reason Joe had developed his voracious love for the outdoors and wildlife.

Touching the eagle talon that hung from the leather cord about his neck, Joe muttered, "You won't die in vain, Max." He'd been allowed to take the talisman from Max's things after the lab had cleared it as free from poison. The talon had been given to Max by his grandfather; a talisman earned because he had been a healer. It had been cherished by Max.

But the tracks to whoever had poisoned Max—and the reason why—were muddled. Did Max have enemies? Not that Joe had been aware of. He'd strayed from close tribal friendships and had been a lone wolf the last few decades. Not harming any living soul, leaving peaceably. A life well lived, and yet, it had been cut short.

The thought to tie Max's alleged murder to the poaching investigation only clicked when Joe remembered Max once muttering that he knew exactly who poached in the county, and that they would get their own someday. Joe had mentioned a family name, and Max's jaw had tightened in confirmation. Everyone knew the Davis family did as they pleased, and poaching was only one of many illegal activities in which they engaged—and got away with.

Now he needed new evidence, a break in the investigation, that would confirm his suspicion. So far, the Davis family had been elusive and covered their tracks like the seasoned tracker-hunters Joe knew they were.

The police radio crackled on the dashboard, and Dispatch reported an incident close to Joe.

"Anyone else respond?" he replied. Generally, if the disturbance was not directly related to fish and game, Dispatch sent out county law enforcement.

"We've got two officers in the area, but both are at the iron mine cave-in."

This morning a closed taconite mine had reported a cave-in. It was believed three overzealous explorers who had crossed the barbed wire fence closing off the mine could be trapped inside.

"No problem," Joe said. "I can handle it. What's the call?"

"Skylar Davis reports she's been shot at on her property. Her address is—"

"I got it." Joe shoved the canteen onto the passenger seat and turned the key in the ignition. His heart suddenly thundered. He knew Skylar Davis. Too well. "Is she hurt?"

"Not sure," Dispatch reported. "Sounded pretty calm on the call. You know where she lives?"

"I'm ten minutes from her land," he said. "I'm on my way."

He spun the truck around on the gravel road and headed east toward the lake where Merlin Davis—brother of Malcolm Davis, who owned Davis Trucking—had owned land for decades. Skylar had inherited her father's land years ago after cancer had taken his life. His daughter now lived alone on hundreds of forested acreage set at the edge of the Boundary Waters Canoe Area. She was a strong woman. A beautiful woman.

She was…the woman Joe could never sweep out of his thoughts. The one who had gotten away.

And she'd been shot at?

He slammed his foot onto the accelerator.

SKYLAR OPENED THE door and sucked in a gasp. Joseph Cash stood on the front stoop, dark hair swept over one eye and looking smart in his uniform. The forest-green short-sleeved shirt and slacks served to enhance his tan skin. Hand at his hip where a gun was holstered, he had been looking aside until she'd stepped onto the threshold. When he turned to her and his stunning green eyes connected with hers, she clasped a hand over her heart.

"Skylar, are you all right?" She heard genuine concern in his urgent tone.

She had so many things she wanted to say to him. Yet at the moment, she didn't know how to assemble a coherent sentence. Joseph Cash was the kindest person she'd known, and had always seemed to be there when she'd needed protecting. Be it in high school when she'd been bullied for sitting at the unpopular kids' table, or even when she'd had to struggle for customers when she'd been working as a small-animal veterinarian in town and most took their animals to the big city of Duluth. And yet, despite his kindnesses, she'd pushed Joe away, wanting to prove to him that she was her own woman. Independent and strong. That she didn't need a man to look over her.

Her rushed choice in fiancé had proved just that point. What a fool she had been.

"Joe," she said. "I didn't expect you. I called the county sheriff. I thought…"

"Well, you got me." He cast her a smile that surely

made every woman in the county swoon. But Skylar had never known how to react to his easy charm and shyness, save with a thrust back of her shoulders and, admittedly, a stupidly stubborn need to prove herself.

"I was close when the call came in," he offered. "Just down the road coming off Lake Vaillant after a patrol. You okay, Skylar? Dispatch reports you were shot at? What's going on?"

"I'm okay. And yes, I believe I was shot at." She absently stroked her fingers over her ear, covering it with her loose blond hair. "I didn't expect you," she said again, rather dumbly.

Because if she had known Joseph Cash would be the one standing on her front stoop, she might have brushed on a little blush and combed her hair. At the very least, changed into some clean jeans.

A squawk from behind Joe made him turn sharply on the creaky lower wood step. Skylar noticed his hand instinctively went to his hip where his gun was holstered. A chicken in a pink knit sweater scampered across the crushed quartz pebbles that paved the stone walk up to the front steps.

"What the hell?" Joe said.

"That's Becky. She wants you to see her. She's very concerned about her looks. Do you like her sweater?"

The man scratched his head and then bobbed it in a nod, even while squinting questionably. "Yes?"

"She's one of my rehab residents."

"That's right, you rehabilitate animals. I'm not even going to ask about the sweater." He followed the chicken's retreat across the yard until she scrambled around the side of the house.

"Uh…come inside." Skylar stepped back and allowed him to enter the log cabin where she'd been living for two years.

When her father passed, the family land had become her possession, as she was his only child. At least, it was hers according to a handwritten note Merlin Davis had written a week before his death. Skylar had lived in the house until she'd moved to Duluth for college. Eventually, she'd made her way back to the town of Checker Hill and set up shop as the resident veterinarian. She'd never gotten much business. The townspeople were leery of the name Davis. Now this home felt too big for one person, but it was a comfort to nestle onto the aged leather sofa in the evenings, blanket wrapped about her shoulders, and admire the photos of her and her dad that she kept on each and every wall.

"You want something to drink? I've got lemonade."

Joe grabbed her by the upper arm to stop her from fleeing across the open floor plan living area and into the kitchen.

"What is it?" She shrugged out of his grasp with a huff. He looked concerned now. Too much so. She didn't want any man's pity.

"Seriously? Skylar, I'm not here for lemonade. I'm here to make sure you're okay. And not bleeding." He looked from her head down to her shoulders and all the way to her feet, then back up again. "And—where did the shots come from? Do you know who it was? How long has it been? I should go outside and take a look around. It's this way, right?"

He headed through the living area and skirted the long quartz kitchen counter. Toward the back of the house sat the screened-in sunporch that stretched the width of the cabin and overlooked the lake. Once before, he'd been in this cabin. When her father had been dying, he'd come to pay his respects. But how dare he traipse on through—

Skylar stopped herself from reprimanding him. He was here on duty. And she had called the police for help, much as her better judgment had screamed for her not to. Would she hear about this from her uncle? On the other hand, maybe Malcolm Davis already knew about the incident. And, yes, that thought sickened Skylar.

"Just through the sliding doors," she called to Joe. "You can take the deck stairs down to the backyard."

After grabbing her cowboy hat, which rested on the back of the couch and which she wore like any other woman might wear earrings or a favorite necklace, she followed the man's bowlegged pace out to the deck.

Standing on the high wood deck, which was stilted ten feet up due to the slope of the ground below, Joe took in everything. The perimeter of the yard was round, echoing out from the firepit in the center. Surrounding the yard were striped hostas that grew thick and lush in the shade provided by the paper birch and sugar maple.

He took the stairs down to the ground. "Where were you? Were you burning a fire?"

He walked over to the fire pit and peered over it. Burnt cedar lingered in the air. As well, the grass was speckled with gray ash flakes from her hastily dowsing the flames with the garden hose after calling the sheriff.

Skylar cringed when she noticed the wedding dress was only half burned and melted among the charred logs. She hadn't thought to cover up what she'd been doing. It had been a personal moment. A much-needed ritual of release. A reclaiming of her power.

Joe scratched his head. Hands at his hips, head cocked downward, he stared at the remnants of the dress. Skylar didn't want to answer the question that must be lighting all the circuits in his brain right now.

"Tell me everything," he said. Then he stretched his gaze around the backyard and out toward the lake. "Did you get a look at the shooter? Were they on your property? Cruising by in a boat? Partyers out for a spin on the lake?"

"I don't know." Skylar walked over to the smoldering fire pit and stood beside the hitching post, which she utilized as a stand to hang roasting sticks and an emergency water bucket she always kept filled when she was burning.

"I was burning a few things. And… I was about here." She stepped to the right a few feet and Joe turned to eye her intently. Dark stubble shadowed his jaw. The golden evening light, beaming through the tree canopy, granted his eyes a rich emerald cast. Everything about the man was intense, dark and—waiting on her.

"Yes, here," she decided, stomping her boot toe into the grass. "I was talking to Stella—"

"There was someone else here?"

"Stella, my wolf."

"Your…wolf?" He hooked his hands in the back pockets of his pants and looked about. "What the—? You took in a wolf cub?"

"Stella has been with me a few years. I found her in a snare trap when she was a pup. I hate it when hunters call those things humane. They are anything but. I took her to the office in town and had to amputate her back leg. Since then, she's flourished. She's not around right now."

Skylar scanned the area. The wolf must be off with the half-dozen chickens—surprisingly, her best friends. Stella was protective of Skylar, but she always left the immediate area when visitors or company arrived. She was a little skittish until she could scent out the newcomer, and then she would eventually put in an appearance.

"I do rehabilitate animals," Skylar pointed out to Joe, who nodded.

"Right. I just thought keeping a wolf as a pet…"

"I have a permit."

"Sure. Still, they are a wild animal." He gave her a side glance that dripped with judgment.

"She had nowhere else to go. I tried to get her to return to the pack, but they wouldn't have it."

"Uh-huh." He wasn't having it, either.

Yes, wolves were wild and should never be kept as pets. Skylar agreed with that wholeheartedly. But when injured and abandoned by their pack, the wolf's only future was living as a loner. And for a pup living out in the wild populated with predators, the fate was most certainly a cruel death.

It didn't matter to her what Joe thought of her choice to keep Stella. Skylar loved her like a family member.

"So you were standing right there and...?" he prompted.

"I was watching the flames, talking to Stella and... at first I felt something on my ear. Thought it was a wicked mosquito bite."

She touched her ear and Joe stepped forward. It was well past the supper hour, and the forest edging her backyard filtered the setting sun, turning it into a hazy twilight. He dug out a small flashlight from a back pocket and shone it on her ear. The man stood so close she could smell his aftershave—something subtle yet masculine with a hint of lemony citronella.

He examined her ear, which had been nicked on the top and had bled minimally. Of course, she'd gasped at the sight of it in the bathroom mirror. She'd never been so close to being killed in her life. And that had angered more than frightened her. What would have become of Stella and the other animals she cared for if she had died? The thought of them being relocated, or worse, was heart wrenching.

As Joe looked her over, she studied his face. There were three Cash brothers, all born and raised in Crooked Creek, a sister town to Checker Hill. There wasn't a female in either of the two close towns who didn't know who they were, because those boys were genetic anomalies, fashion models roughed up by the wild. Sinuous and muscular. So sexy. And Joe's deep green eyes were a thing to behold.

"If that bullet had been half an inch closer..." The man suddenly bowed his head and winced.

Skylar was taken aback by his reaction. "Joe? What's wrong? I'm okay."

"Right." He lifted his head and his jaw pulsed with tension. "You always were able to take care of yourself."

He'd learned exactly what she'd hoped to teach him about her. Regrettably.

Skylar lifted her chin bravely. "Still can take care of myself."

"Being shot at is no way to go about it, Skylar. If anything would have happened to you..." He winced again and looked aside, toward the fire pit.

Skylar found herself leaning forward in hopes of him finishing that sentence. Then again, she suspected how he would finish it. He'd never hidden his interest in her. And she wasn't prepared for such a statement right now.

If only he'd said as much to her two months earlier. Of course, then he'd been avoiding her like the plague.

It was well deserved on her part.

He placed his hands akimbo and scanned the lake. "Do you know what direction the shot was fired from?"

She pointed out through the gap in the bowed birch trees that she'd always thought of as a sort of pulled-back curtain to the stage of the lake. "I feel like it came from that way."

"See anyone down by the shore?"

She shook her head. Then she remembered, and turned to point out the bullet holes that had splintered and pierced the hitching post.

"Two?" Joe bent to study the post with the flashlight. "These are clean, and one goes all the way through." He paused and glanced at her as if to temper his words for her tender ears.

"I'm a big girl, Joe. You can say the bad stuff without offending or scaring me."

"I guess so." He returned his attention to the holes and tapped the post with a finger. "I have some evidence bags in the truck. I'm going to grab them, but I should also call in someone to take some photos and—" His attention veered to the ground behind the post. "Here's a bullet."

He tugged out a black latex glove from his pocket, pulled it on and picked up the bullet from the ground. It was long, and Skylar leaned in to peer at it as he did.

Joe swore.

"What is it?" she asked.

"My dad collects guns, and he taught me and my brothers a lot about the different types and their ammunition. This is most definitely from a high-powered rifle, Skylar."

"I don't understand. Not the usual hunting rifle?"

"Nope. If that had been the case, that hitching post would be pocked with lead shot. As well as you."

Skylar sucked in a breath.

"Sorry. Didn't mean to say that."

She nodded, no longer feeling quite as strong as she wanted to.

Joe turned and again cast a glance across the lake. "I

don't think the shooter was close. Could have been across the lake. Which means this is some serious business."

He turned to face her directly and asked, "What's going on? Why would someone be shooting at you? Skylar, is there something you need to tell me?"

Chapter Three

Joe had rushed to Skylar's home upon getting the call from Dispatch. Simply hearing her name had been all he'd needed to become immersed in those old familiar feelings he always got whenever he thought about the tall, sexy blonde. Feelings he wasn't prepared to let emerge right now, because then he'd have to struggle with what had once felt like heartache.

Hell, who was he kidding? It had been, and still was, heartache.

Save for occasionally spying her walking into the grocery store or out of the local café, he hadn't spoken to her for almost a year. That had been a purposeful avoidance.

Long, tawny blond hair spilled over her shoulders. And that cowboy hat she always wore shaded her blue eyes, but in the rich evening twilight, a flash of sun from across the lake created glints like sapphires in those irises. And when she parted her soft pink lips to speak, Joe's heart thundered.

"I don't know what you think I should know, Joe," she said. "How can I know who was shooting at me?"

Drawn back to the moment, he briefly met her gaze—and almost fell into that heartache again. But he managed to snag a grip on the present and pull himself up and into business mode.

"It's standard procedure to ask a lot of questions after an incident like this," he said. "Any details you can provide that might help me figure this out?" He cast his gaze across the lake again. "It had to have come from across the lake."

"Really? That far away? It's a good three-quarters of a mile to the other side."

"Sniper rifles can hit a target miles away. My brother, Jason, used to be one of the best when he was…well." Jason didn't like his family to talk about the fact he used to be a CIA agent. And most didn't know that he had been. "Not that it was such a rifle. Nothing's been confirmed yet. But whoever made that shot…"

It wasn't right to be impressed at a moment like this, but that was some distance to the other side of the lake. Had to have been a boat driving by.

Skylar blew out a breath, but it had a nervous vibration to it. She suddenly stepped to the side and wobbled. Joe caught her arm and shoulder against his chest and hugged her. The scent of pine and lemons teased his nose. He slid a hand down to her waist and across her back to offer her a sturdy hold.

"You okay?"

She nodded, but her expression indicated she was far from okay.

"Let's get you inside. I don't think it's wise to stand out here."

"You think they could still be out there? It's been over an hour."

"Unlikely." He helped her walk toward the deck. "But you could use a cup of tea or something."

"Brandy," she said, then laughed. "Oh, Joe, I guess it did throw me. I was fine after I called the police. But now…"

As they approached the deck stairs, a dog came padding out from the forest that edged the north side of the house.

But wait. That was no dog.

"Stella has finally decided you pass muster." Skylar gripped the deck railing and sat on the second step from the bottom. "Just give me a minute, will you?"

"Of course." While Skylar sat to settle her nerves, Joe whistled to the approaching animal. "A timber wolf."

"She's my rescue sweetie. Hey, Stella."

The beautiful wolf approached on light footsteps, her gold eyes and coal nose aimed for Joe. Her tail was held slightly erect, with a bit of a kink to it. Warning, but cautiously optimistic. He'd known that Skylar had found a wolf pup in a trap a few years ago, and thought she'd rehabilitated it and sent it off to its pack. But to keep it as a pet?

By instinct, he dropped to one knee and bowed his head as Stella neared. One thing a human should never do was look a wolf directly in the eye. It was a sign of challenge and authority that he dared not risk with this unfamiliar wolf. He noticed a slight hop to her step. She managed very well on three legs.

Raising his head, Joe held out his hand but did not stretch toward the curious animal. She would sniff him out, decide what she thought about him. As she had likely been doing when she'd been hiding in the woods. A wolf's sense of smell was far superior to that of a dog's. Stella had already decided whether he was friend or foe. Because of that, he felt honored that she'd come out to greet him.

The wolf approached on careful footsteps, stretching out her neck to sniff at Joe's fingers. Her tail unkinked and waggled slightly.

"I spent a lot of time with her in the early months," Skylar commented from the step. "Nearly twenty-four/ seven, sleeping with her on a mattress for weeks, acclimating her to my human self and letting her know I would not harm her."

She'd taken the right steps for a wolf to live with humans. But Joe always favored reintroducing the animal back into the wild before such drastic measures were taken. On the other hand, if her pack had abandoned her, as they may do to the sick or wounded, he could be thankful Skylar had been there for her.

"I suspect her mother was killed. Otherwise, I'm sure she would have stayed around her pup in the trap."

"Very possible. Wolves will never be pets," Joe said quietly. "They will always have the wild in them. Right, Stella?"

The wolf's tongue lashed his fingers, and he let out the breath he had been holding. Just one lick. She wasn't going to get overly enthusiastic about a new human, but she did seem to trust him. As proof, she allowed him to ruffle his hand over her fur and he went for the sweet spot behind her ear, giving it a light scratch. The wolf sat before him, reveling in the attention he gave her.

"She's beautiful. I'm honored to meet you, Stella. But where's your pack?"

"Pretty sure she was from the Boundary Edge pack," Skylar said. "I checked the records with the wolf center. They hadn't recorded any births, but they don't have twenty-four/seven watch, either. And only one of the pack males is tagged with a tracking device. They were able to tell me about a year after I'd had Stella that one of the females was missing. They hadn't found her body. So I'm sticking with the dead-mother theory. Stella was a long way from home. That pack travels about ten miles north from here."

"I'm familiar with that pack," Joe said. "Well, their territory. Never gotten close to any of them, but I have tracked them before. So Stella was found in a leg trap?"

"It was actually a snare. She was near death. Had been gnawing at her own leg. I waited and watched for other wolves, but there were none close. I figured she was about three months old at the time. It's been almost three years. She'll never be mine, but I am her person. I did take her to the pack rendezvous point about a month after she'd been with me. Not a single wolf showed."

"They were watching," Joe guessed. "But by then Stella was marked by human scent." He combed his fingers through Stella's soft summer pelt. The brown, gray and black fur had likely received a good combing from Skylar, for he didn't notice any unpreened winter undercoat. She lifted her head, luxuriating in his touch. "That's too bad. She would thrive with others of her kind."

"She's not doing so terribly with me."

"No, she's not. Looks healthy and happy."

The wolf tilted her head against his head and he took a moment to relish the contact. It was rare he got to experience the wild so close. And, yes, she was still wild. He'd wager any man who came toward Skylar with intent to harm, or whom Stella hadn't properly sniffed out, would risk a bite or worse.

"You haven't started your own pack, have you, Skylar?"

"Of my own design. I rehabilitate all breeds here. Goats, chickens, cats and snakes. Even had a baby moose once, but thankfully, she went back to her mother. Stella was my first and so far only wolf. Which reminds me, I have to run into town tomorrow to pick up some red yarn."

"For rehabilitation purposes?"

"You met Becky. She wants a change of sweater. Very fashion forward, that chicken."

Somewhere on the edge of the yard, a goat bleated.

"Beyoncé knows we're talking about her," Skylar offered. "She's a dancer."

Joe didn't even know how to respond, so he let that one pass without comment.

Now Stella licked his face. So he sat on the ground and she stepped forward onto his legs. The wolf was big, perhaps eighty pounds, but not as big as some could get in the wild. Standing on their back legs, a wolf could rise well over a tall man's head. Their weight could range from seventy to one hundred fifty pounds, and they were strong and powerful. Stella seemed amiable, willing to accept him.

"This is the first time she's ever welcomed a stranger so freely," Skylar said. "There's always been something special about you, Joe. I think you're a wolf whisperer."

Joe shook his head. She'd never teasingly called him Nature Boy, as his older brothers were apt to, which he appreciated. It was a nickname that had stuck since that fateful weekend he'd gotten lost in the Boundary Waters. Just thinking about it brought up memories of Max Owen, and that forced Joe back to the present. Because he would not let Max's bizarre death be ignored without discovering the reason behind it.

"I just like animals," he offered. "All animals. And I respect them. They have souls and are more a part of this land than we will ever be. But enough of the greeting—we have to get your person inside," he said to Stella. "She's been through a lot. And I want to head across the lake to look around."

As Joe stood, the wolf followed, watching him guide Skylar up the stairs by her arm. She was reluctant to accept the assistance—he could sense her tug in resistance—but finally she relented and her body hugged his as he walked her across the deck toward the patio doors.

Skylar Davis possessed an independent streak deeper than his ability to express his true feelings toward her. They'd known one another since high school, and he'd pined over her from afar since then. They'd become friends as sophomores—biology class had paired them over a frog dissection—and following high school, college had separated them for years. But they'd both found their way back to Checker Hill, and one another. A few years ago, they had decided to take a chance at dating. Thing was, their schedules had never meshed, and each time Joe had asked Skylar if she was free, she had been seeing someone else. Vice versa, for one time she'd asked him out when he'd been dating a girl from Duluth.

There had been that time at a wedding reception for a mutual friend. They'd both been drunk. And, well, what had ensued that night—or rather, hadn't—had changed things between them.

And then Joe's best friend had stepped into the picture and had turned Skylar's head completely away from Joe. And that was the reason he hadn't spoken to her in a year.

Joe cast a glance down toward the extinguished fire pit. A wedding dress lay smoldering in bits and pieces. He'd like to ask about that, but he'd wait for a better time.

SKYLAR WATCHED AS Joe pulled onto the long, pine-bordered driveway that curled out to the county road. He intended to cruise to the other side of the lake and take a look around. All in a day's police work, she felt sure. Impressive, since she was aware he'd worked a full shift today and she'd thought conservation officers generally stuck to checking hunting licenses and beach patrol.

No, she knew that wasn't right. The conservation officers in the Boundary Waters had their hands full with poaching, theft of natural resources, search and rescue of lost hikers, and they were even called in to consult on murder cases when a body was found in the woods. They carried all the usual authority and powers a police officer would.

Much as she hadn't expected Joe to knock on her door this evening, she was thankful now that it had been him. Because she needed…something. Help? Support? This keeping her mouth shut about the minor indiscretions Davis Trucking employees committed and hoping her relationship with her uncle would improve was getting her nowhere.

Still, Malcolm had offered to buy a section of her land. Then she'd have seed money to build the shelter. But at what price was her alliance to her uncle? Would her dad have wanted that? He'd kept the land pristine. Had always refused to sell to his brother so he could fulfill plans to expand the business. Malcolm had no love for the environment, while Merlin, Skylar's dad, had been a certified tree hugger.

And now she'd been threatened. Seriously. She could have been killed. Had the threat come from Malcolm? That didn't make sense. If he wanted to buy her land he should be kissing up to her. And yet…

Two days ago, Skylar had stumbled onto something she shouldn't have seen. She wasn't sure what had been in those freezers in the Davis Trucking warehouse, but the man with a rifle in hand who'd discovered her had not been happy to see her.

What to do?

Because, much as Uncle Malcolm had stood for the

opposite of everything her father had, he was still family. And family meant something to her.

But family didn't fire warning shots at one another.

Chapter Four

The drive around the lake did not bring Joe to the spot where he'd determined the shooter might have been standing. Calling for backup, he got an answer from a state patrol. An officer could be around in twenty minutes. Joe predicted a hike through the woods to get to the position across from the lake to the Davis home, so he waited for the patrol officer to arrive. Otherwise, they'd never find each other in the thick pine and birch forest that offered only narrow trails here and there.

As a conservation officer, he spent 90 percent of his time roaming the woods and lakes in his territory. He knew this area. But he hadn't spent much time on this lake. It was small and usually only boated by the residents living around it.

Antsy, and wishing he'd taken an hour in the gym this morning to work out, he bounced on his feet. His hiking boots were not the most comfortable for such movement, but he liked to stay limber. He snapped up his knee and kicked out in a Muay Thai move that could knock an opponent flat.

He'd developed an interest in martial arts from

watching his mother practice her moves from the karate class she'd taken when her boys were younger. He'd started with karate, but after watching a few *National Geographic* specials and sports TV, he'd fallen in love with the ultrahigh kicks and swift elbow strikes Muay Thai offered. It was all about brute power. It worked his body in every way possible, and kept him limber and sharp. And a well-honed body only enhanced an ever-growing soul. He was constantly learning. His greatest teachers? Nature and the wildlife he had taken an oath to protect.

But honestly? It was a good means to get out his anger by kicking the sandbag now and then.

Pausing at the harsh, croaking call of a blue heron, Joe lifted his head and closed his eyes. He had to smile at that sound. Such utter peace here, away from the city and major highways. He opened his eyes, scanning the treetops in hopes of seeing the heron nest, but the canopy was thick. The last slivers of sunlight glinted like stars.

A car honked and Joe waved to the approaching patrol car. Brent Kofax was with the sheriff's department. In cases where someone had been shot, or threatened, they usually joined the investigation. He stepped out of the car and gave Joe a thumbs-up. Joe had worked with Brent on a few occasions when backup was necessary. Usually when he knew he'd be approaching a boat full of drunk fishermen, or that one time Joe had needed someone to help him sort out steel traps from a burned-out Quonset building.

"What do you have tonight, Cash?"

Joe shook Brent's hand and pointed over his shoulder toward the lake. "The Davis woman who lives across the lake was shot at earlier this evening. Judging by the trajectory of the hit, I'm guessing the shooter might have been in the woods about a quarter mile up. I need another set of eyes. You ready to do some hiking?"

"I always know you'll give me a workout when I answer your calls. Already changed into hiking boots. Let's do this!"

From his car Joe grabbed a backpack that contained evidence-collection supplies, water and snacks, as well as a compass and other survival equipment. He never ventured into the woods without it. At his hip, he wore his pistol, a Glock .40 caliber. Brent carried a 12-gauge pump shotgun, standard issue nowadays.

The two men picked carefully through the brush and grasses, dodging roots and ducking low-hanging pine tree branches. Brent was an avid hunter, unlike Joe, but he wouldn't criticize the man's need to kill innocent animals for food. The day he started doing that was the day he volunteered to have his life held under a microscope and examined for faults. He had many, but cruelty to animals was not one of them. His anti-hunting stance got him some razzing from his fellow conservation officers. They tended to think that COs with wildlife management training let their love for nature get in the way of their police work. The opposite was true. Joe protected the citizens as well as the animals.

They hiked half a mile through thick pine and aspen. The sun had set, and he and Brent were now using flashlights, but the moon was three-quarters full and there was still some ambient light glimmering off the calm lake water. Thanks to Joe's sharp eye, they found a deer trail, as well as scat droppings under some fallen maple leaves. Their path kept them within a thirty-foot distance from the lake shore. The shooter would have gotten close enough to the edge of the forest for a good, clear shot, Joe decided. Thankful for the beaten-down brush, he tracked until he spotted shell casings. Ballistic evidence. Excellent.

They stood twenty feet in from the lakeshore, well camouflaged by tall brush and a frond of wild fern. With shell casings just behind him, and the grass trampled down around them, Joe figured this was where the shooter had been positioned. He studied the ground, which was folded-down marsh grass and moss. If it had been dirt, he might have found impressions from a tripod the shooter would have surely utilized to hold steady aim and sight in the Davis property nearly a mile across the lake, as well as shoe tracks.

"You never cease to amaze me," Brent commented as he bent to shine his flashlight on the shell casings. "What? Did you grow up in the woods like Mowgli, or something?"

"I think Mowgli lived in the jungle," Joe commented. But there had been a time, in his family, when his brothers had referred to him as Mowgli, until they'd decided on the more annoying Nature Boy.

It wasn't often a boy found himself lost in the woods for three days, and was finally led out and home by a pack of wolves. That experience had changed Joe's life. First, his parents had hugged him and showered him with kisses. Then, they'd grounded him for wandering off by himself without taking a cell phone along, despite the fact that it wasn't easy to call home in the middle of the Boundary Waters where cell towers were few and far between. But Joe had taken the punishment and had used it to study up on wolves, and from that day forward his direction had been clear. He wanted to work with wildlife and protect them from the hazards of living so close to humans.

"You got an evidence kit in that backpack?" Brent asked. "I left mine in the car." He stood and flashed his beam around where they stood, hooking his rifle up on a shoulder.

"Always." Taking a pair of black latex gloves out of the backpack, Joe collected the two metal shell casings and put them in a plastic bag he usually used for collecting marine specimens from boats docked on lake shores. He'd seen the two bullet holes in the hitching post by the fire pit.

That the first bullet had nicked Skylar's ear told him someone did not want her dead. Whoever had pulled the trigger had skills similar to his brother Jason. To come so close without harming her? Such a shot required nerves of steel and perfect timing.

The second shot must have zinged within a foot of her body. Enough to scare the hell out of anyone. Any woman—or man—would have fainted or run screaming. He'd figured Skylar had taken it calmly, until he'd seen her falter beside the fire pit. He'd left her sipping brandy with Stella curled at her feet. She'd insisted she didn't want protection overnight, but Joe considered sending out a patrol officer to park down the long drive that led to her property.

Or he might do that himself. He'd been up since five, had hit the lake at six and had spent a hot day out on the water. It was late now, and he was exhausted, but he knew he wouldn't sleep if he left Skylar alone. He'd park at the end of the drive, and she'd never be the wiser. There were worse ways to spend a summer evening.

As he stood up from collecting the casings, his gaze caught something that was neither flora nor fauna. Brent took a step forward, his attention focused across the lake, and—

Joe swore and lunged into a kick that caught the officer on his hip, hitting none too gently and throwing him off course.

"What the hell, man?" Brent had dropped his flashlight and rifle, and splayed his hands in question before him.

The flashlight rolled and stopped with a clink. Both men looked to the spot where Brent had almost stepped. Joe cautiously approached the oak tree. His flashlight swept the ground, taking it all in, watching for a steel trap. But he knew he wouldn't find it, because the set snare wasn't usually used in tandem with such a trap.

The flashlight beam fell over the snare trap—a light wire cable anchored to the base of the oak. If any animal stepped on that, the loop would tighten about their leg. Or worse—if they sniffed the bait peeking out from under some wet aspen leaves, it would become a noose and string them up, likely breaking their neck. In a worst-case scenario, the noose would not snap and the

animal would be suspended, alive, left to slowly suffo-
cate until the poacher returned.

"Bastards," Joe muttered.

"I almost stepped on that." Brent eased a hand down
his hip where Joe had kicked him. "You could have just
called 'stop.'"

"I owed you one for that upper cut in the gym a few
weeks ago."

Brent chuckled. "Yeah, that was a good one. Pretty
rare I get the upper hand with you."

Joe picked up a branch and used it to nudge the snare.
The trap sprang and released the snare in a flutter of
leaves. Joe would disassemble the entire thing and take
it in to the county forensics lab for a thorough study.
With any luck, they'd find fingerprints.

"You got wire snips in that backpack?" Brent asked
as Joe sorted through his pack. When he proudly displayed just that, Brent shook his head. "Never mind.
Mowgli knows what he's doing."

Yeah, he didn't care for the moniker so much from
people who weren't family. Joe snipped the cable and,
latex gloves still on, untangled it from around the tree
trunk. Brent gathered it into a loop.

The disturbance uncovered a few bits of bait meat.
The smell was rancid, but Joe bagged it as well. The forensic lab could determine a lot from testing bait meat,
such as the animal it had come from, and possibly even
pick up some fingerprints. Briefly, he wondered if the
meat was poisoned. It was an important detail that he
wouldn't have proof of until tests had been run.

Stuffing the evidence bags into his backpack, Joe

stood and looked out over the chrome-and-hematite-sheened lake. His investigation into the poaching hadn't taken him quite this far south. Now he'd expand that range. First, he needed to check whose land this was. He'd thought it was state owned, but he couldn't be sure until he checked a map.

The poachers weren't even sneaky; they seemed to be growing bolder every month, leaving traps everywhere. And the thing that had tipped Joe off initially had been an ad on Craigslist. Selling deer antlers and bear claws online? Blatant.

Yet he hadn't run into the poison that had been found in Max's system, even with the samples he'd sent in to the lab. He could be way off course in trying to connect the man's death with the local poachers, but Joe sensed he was on the right track. Every bone in his body pushed him to continue with the search for Max's killer. The man had not been accidentally poisoned. No one handled strychnine without taking precautions.

And now there was a new twist to the investigation. Could the one who had set this snare have been the one who'd shot at Skylar? It couldn't be coincidence that the shooting site was so close to a trap.

Joe narrowed his gaze across the calm dark waters. A small light showed from what was probably Skylar's living room. He hoped she would sleep well, with the wolf keeping guard outside. But he didn't guess Stella would provide protection, and he wouldn't expect it. The animal seemed skittish and hesitant to approach strangers, and that wasn't a bad thing. But that meant Skylar was not safe.

And yet, why would a poacher shoot at her? It had to have been some kind of warning. Did she know something that someone wanted her to keep silent about? And if it had been a warning, whoever had fired would have known his target would take it as a warning.

Which meant Skylar might know more than she was letting on.

"Lieutenant Brock said something about finding illegal guns in an Ely residence." Brent looped the coiled cable over his forearm.

"I found a cache of guns with the serial numbers filed off last week," Joe offered. "They were in a shed with a dozen illegal deer racks."

Brent shook his head. "You need help with any of it?"

Joe nodded. "Always. You can take this in to the county forensics van, for a start."

"I'm heading toward Ely. I think Elaine Hester is on shift tonight. Smart chick. What are you up to now?"

"Headed back across the lake."

He needn't tell Brent he had decided to stand vigil outside the target's home because he feared losing her more than his heart could stand.

STEPPING OUT OF the shower, Skylar dried off, then reached for the brandy goblet on the vanity. She downed the last two swallows. Whew! That burned. But she instantly felt the calming effects ease through her muscles, and the need to close her eyes and drop into a heavy sleep.

"Come on, Stella."

She padded naked down the hallway to her bedroom,

followed by the three-legged wolf. Stella generally slept outside, but she would never ignore an invite to stay indoors. The security panel for the entire house was positioned at eye level in the bedroom, by the door. She turned on all the door locks and the perimeter alarm, which was set only for the weight of a vehicle since she had so many animals wandering around at any given time.

Stella jumped onto the end of her bed. Her spot. And let no man try to prove otherwise.

Pulling on a long T-shirt that hung past her thighs, Skylar crawled onto the bed and lay on top of the sheets across the middle of the mattress, so she could smooth her palm over Stella's fur.

She hadn't seen Joseph Cash in…must be a year. He got more handsome every time she saw him. He had the "tall, dark stranger" thing going on full force. Except he wasn't a stranger, and…she wanted to see him again.

Under better circumstances than getting shot at.

"It was a warning," she whispered, tracing the top of her ear, which felt tender from the bruise. She caught a swallow at the back of her throat, followed by a single teardrop slipping down the side of her face.

She'd walked into a warehouse on Davis Trucking land, and before calling out for her uncle, she'd glanced around. There were crates everywhere, marked with company names. Standard inventory for a trucking outfit, she figured. But the freezers, six of them, had stood out. They were the large white chest kind, probably close to twenty cubic feet in volume.

What had been in them? With a trucking business,

it could be anything. And while she'd always assumed they didn't store goods on-site, she didn't know enough about the operation.

A man standing over one of the opened freezers hadn't noticed her, so she'd cleared her throat. He'd lifted his head and swung a look over his shoulder, focusing his gaze on her. She hadn't recognized him, and he'd immediately slammed down the freezer cover and grabbed a rifle. The feeling of utter dread had overcome her. Skylar had turned and run. As she had, he'd called after her, "Don't tell, bitch! This is none of your concern."

She'd run straight to her truck, past a few truckers who had called out to her and whistled. The stranger hadn't followed her. Forget talking to her uncle. She'd been creeped out, and had put her truck in gear and gotten the hell out of there.

She hadn't told anyone. Because she wasn't sure what she had seen. But it had been something. Because tonight they had warned her.

And yet, she'd dared to call the police. Because she would not be scared off by some idiot assholes who thought they had a right to threaten a woman. Hell, the shooter could have killed her.

Now, dare she ask Joseph Cash to protect her?

Chapter Five

Joe woke and winced. He was sitting at an angle—ah, hell. He'd fallen asleep in the truck parked at the end of Skylar's driveway.

The rapping noise that had woken him thumped again on his window. Sliding upright in the driver's seat, he moaned at the tug to his aching back muscles, then managed a blinking glance to his left. And then he opened his eyes wide and took in the view.

Could a woman look more beautiful in a cowboy hat, no makeup and plain denim shirt unbuttoned to just there? He voted no. She was like sunshine and all those pretty things guys liked to look at but were always afraid to touch for fear of smearing them with dirt or breaking something delicate.

Skylar Davis was not a delicate woman. She'd made that clear to him over the years he'd known her. And he expected some stern words to follow the admonishing look she was giving him now.

Turning the keys in the ignition, Joe pushed the window button, which slid down slowly. "Mornin', Skylar."

"Really, Joe? Did you sleep out here all night?"

"Most of the time? Nope. Wasn't sleeping. I was on watch. Must have fallen asleep a few hours ago." He wasn't sure what time it was and glanced at the dashboard. Seven o'clock. He may have gotten two hours' sleep at most. The night had been spent with the radio turned low to the '90s top hits, his eyes half-closed, as he'd kept an eye toward the Davis house.

"I told you I didn't need looking after."

"Just doing my job, Skylar. You were in danger last night. It's not clear that danger has passed. I wouldn't be a very good law enforcement officer if I'd walked away and left you vulnerable. How'd you sleep? Where's Stella?"

"She's playing with Becky. And I'm headed into town on errands."

"Right. Pink yarn, wasn't it?"

"Red. That, and groceries. Will you move your truck so I can drive through? Or are you now a permanent fixture that I have to learn to live with like some kind of skin growth?"

Someone was not a morning person. Still, her pretty eyes made up for that touch of rancor. "Listen, Skylar, I know you don't care for me—"

"My feelings for you have nothing to do with what's going on right now, so don't bring that into the situation."

She had *feelings* for him? Joe raked his fingers through his hair and sat up a little straighter.

"I appreciate you investigating the shooting," she said. "And I understand you'll have further questions for me. I'll cooperate as much as I can. But I already gave you my statement."

"As much as you can?" Joe opened the car door and stepped out. Another tug at his back muscles reminded him how little time he spent sitting all night in a car keeping a vigilant watch for intruders. "What's going on, Skylar? I feel like you know something you're not willing to tell me. Or are you afraid? Is that it? Is someone threatening you?"

"Of course I was threatened!"

"Yes, but why? If it was a threat, then generally the person being threatened has an idea about why."

She crossed her arms tightly over her chest, paced to the front of his truck and then swung out her arms in surrender. "It's not what you think, Joe. I just… Did you find the place where the shooter may have been positioned?"

"I did. As predicted, I found a couple shell casings. Sent them in to forensics for analysis."

Now she gave him her full attention. Sunlight flashed through the tree canopy, gleaming on her smooth skin. That someone had wanted to hurt her, or at the very least threaten her, tightened Joe's resolve to find the culprit. No woman, especially Skylar, should ever be put in such a position of fear.

"I found a snare, set and waiting to spring."

Skylar nodded subtly, taking it in. She didn't seem surprised. And for as rampant as poaching was in the Superior Forest, it wasn't as if most people ever encountered such a situation unless they went looking for it, as a conservation officer would.

"You ever catch poachers on your land, Skylar?"

"Catch them? No. I'd be a fool to go after an idiot with a gun and the mentality that animals are there for the taking, no matter the pain they cause the poor creatures."

Joe nodded. They were of the same mind regarding treatment of animals. All animals. Not just the ones society had designated as pets.

"Most of the land owners around here carry a gun," he said. "And while the majority are law-abiding and only hunt with a license, there are those idiots, as you call them, who think they can do as they please. I've been investigating a poaching ring close to this area for months."

"Is that so?"

He nodded. She was interested, but she was also holding back on the conversation. She knew something. He sensed it. Could she have information that might lead him to whoever had poisoned Max?

"You know it's your duty to report poaching activity, Skylar."

"I know that."

"Don't approach the culprit, just get a name or description, location of the trap or snare, and call it in."

"I can do that. And I will. If I ever happen upon something like that."

"You gotta be careful trekking through these woods."

"This *is* my property."

"Is it clearly marked? Fenced?"

"No." She hooked a hand at her hip and lifted her chin. "My father had a good relationship with all the area families. We all respect boundaries and will often allow one another to hunt on our land, with permission. I've never had a problem…"

Joe waited as her words seemed to hang. She wasn't saying something, and he really wanted to wrench it out of her, but he didn't want to play hardball and force their relationship into something uncomfortable for her.

Not that they had a relationship. Well, beyond that he'd considered her a friend up until a year ago.

"What about your uncle?" he prompted. He knew Malcolm Davis's land hugged Merlin Davis's—now Skylar's—land in some manner. It had all originally been owned by their father, Skylar's grandfather.

"What about him?" Skylar now studied the ground intently.

Joe shrugged. "I see Davis Trucking driving the highways all the time. In Duluth, too."

"They are the third biggest trucking company in northern Minnesota. I'm sure they have a loading dock on Superior."

"Been around forever, too. You have a good relationship with them?"

"Davis Trucking? I can't say it's good, bad or ugly."

"I mean your uncle Malcolm. Didn't I hear something about him and your dad having a feud of some sort? I think you mentioned that to me once."

"My dad has been gone for two years, Joe. Leave the past in the past."

"Sorry." He shoved his hands into his back pockets.

That had been a cruel means to try to get more about Malcolm Davis out of her. The patriarch of Davis Trucking was on Joe's suspect list. But he'd yet to get hard evidence on him, save a few random deer pelts and a couple bald eagle talons found in one of his truckers' glove compartments.

"I have to get to the store," Skylar said, interrupting his thoughts. "It's still early, and I have some mowing to do, plus I need to move the chicken house. I like to do that before the hot afternoon sun beats down. You going to move your truck?"

"I will. But I do have more questions. They can wait until after I've had a better look at the evidence. I'm not going to stand back and let you face alone whatever the hell is going on, Skylar. Just a warning. I'm here for you. Like it or not."

She nodded and looked aside. "Sure thing, Joe. Thanks," she said on a tight whisper. "Talk to you soon."

She turned and strode off toward the cabin. Her long legs moved her swiftly, as did her swinging arms. No-nonsense wrapped in a tease of femininity. Had Cole Pruitt really married her? Last Joe had heard, the date had been set. And that wedding dress. So many questions he'd like to have answered.

"She's hiding something," Joe muttered.

And that hurt him almost as much as losing his chance at dating her had. Was she involved with the poachers his investigations were centered around? It was a quick and harsh judgment, but it was something he'd have to consider. She was a member of the Davis family, after all.

"Don't do this to me, Skylar," he said as he slid back behind the wheel of his truck. "I have too much respect for you."

Skylar paid for the two bags of groceries—pleased the small market offered sundries such as the red yarn—then grabbed the bags and headed out to her truck parked in the grassy lot in front of the store. The old Ford she drove had once been red, but the paint job had faded over the years to a rust-mottled pink. Cole had been good with the small fixes it had needed. That was about the only thing she missed about not having him around.

She set the paper bags on the passenger seat and closed the door to walk around to the back, where she paused and leaned against the tailgate to watch passing cars. She was no longer in an irritated mood caused by thoughts of Joseph Cash and his soulful green eyes. Because, mercy, that man had cornered the market on sexy.

Why had she never hooked up with him?

They almost had that one night. And then...

And then. The big rejection from him. That still hurt a little. Even though she could understand where he'd been coming from—she being drunker than a skunk. And he had been toasted, as well. That he'd had the mental fortitude to refuse her suggestion of sex was either because he was a strange beast or because he hadn't been as interested in her as she'd thought.

Either way, at the time, his refusal had humiliated her. After that, she'd thought pushing him away was the smart thing to do. Really, the idea of being happy and in love with any man had only driven her mad after losing her father. He'd been torn apart when her mom had left. Skylar had been twelve that morning she'd found a note from her mother placed directly on top of her bowl of shredded wheat. She'd missed the school bus after reading the two sentences: *I can't do this anymore. I love you, Skylar. Mom.*

And she hadn't seen or heard from her since. No check-in calls. No Christmas cards. Not even a "hey, I'm still alive, don't worry about me" message on the phone. Her teenage years had been depressing. Skylar had once been confident and self-assured in her school-work, but middle school had been merely going through the motions. By her sophomore year, Skylar had decided to put her anger into her schoolwork and had graduated a year early. As if that would show her mom.

It hadn't, but it was how she'd coped with the situation. If her mom didn't need her, then she certainly didn't need her, either.

But her father had not been the same after his wife left. He'd refused to even date after that, telling Skylar Dorothy had been his soul mate. On his deathbed he had smiled and whispered Dorothy's name before drifting away.

The woman had not deserved such reverence. Had she ever appreciated her husband's love for her? That was a question Skylar wanted an answer to, but she knew it would never come. So she'd moved forward, and was doing as well as she could now that her dad was gone. Life had felt empty for a while after his death, but her focus on the animals she rehabilitated had worked like a jolt of life infused into her system. She didn't need anyone to make her happy. Nor did she want to risk falling for someone and having them walk out of her life.

Yet now Joe was back in her life, bedroom eyes peering at her suspiciously. The man was investigating a poaching ring? Skylar had to think only one second to guess who might be on his suspect list.

"Damn it." She closed her eyes. "With Joe involved, this is not going to be easy."

She hadn't been surprised to learn Joe had found a live snare close to the shooter's position. She'd seen snares and traps while walking her property. If she'd confessed that to Joe, he would have battered her with questions, all of which would lead to her uncle.

"I don't need this craziness," she said. "I just want a peaceful, simple life. Is that too much to ask?"

Just her and her animals. The three-legged wolf and the naked chicken whose saving grace was a single white tail feather she preened scrupulously. The trio of piglets who had been born underweight were currently thriving. Add to that the occasional dancing goat or family of orphaned baby opossums, and her life had been going smoothly. All she wanted was to build the shelter barn for her menagerie and set up an office for her veterinary supplies, plus a small operating room, and help those animals that she could.

Her cell phone rang, and Skylar answered.

"Miss Davis? I was given your name as someone who might be able to help."

She got calls that began like this often. With no vet in Checker Hills proper, the DNR knew she was the one who took in animals in need of rehabilitation. The alternative was to transport the animal to Duluth, more than an hour away.

"What's up?"

"I've got a baby boa constrictor on my front stoop."

That wasn't exactly her area of expertise. And it wasn't a reptile native to Minnesota. Which meant it had to be some pet that had gotten loose or been abandoned after the owner realized how difficult it was to care for an exotic animal.

"Did you call Animal Control? They're the ones who can wrangle it and remove it from your property."

"Yes, and they're on their way. It's something else I thought you could help me with."

"And what is that?"

"The snake gave one of my old farm cats a good squeeze, and she's in a bad way. Broken ribs for sure. I'm not sentimental about animals. Generally might be inclined to put the poor thing out of her misery. But this one, well, she was my beloved wife's favorite. Olivia died two months ago, bless her heart. And I can't bear to see the cat go now."

"Give me your address," Skylar said. "I'll be right there."

She was a sucker for a sad tale. Also, the distraction would be just what she needed to keep her mind from Joseph Cash and the poaching that she knew was taking place on her land.

Tucking away her cell phone, she turned and walked right into Malcolm Davis. Stepping back, she assessed his cool smile, shaded by the Panama hat he always wore. His face was long and bony, much as her father's had been. In fact, the two men had often been mistaken as twins, despite their two-year age difference.

"Uncle Malcolm, I didn't see you there."

She glanced across the lot. She didn't see his big black diesel truck anywhere. The man drove ostentatious vehicles, but his simple clothing and ordinary manner tended to throw her off, because he was anything but unassuming. Rather caustic, truth be told.

"How have you been, Skylar? Haven't seen you for a while."

It had been days since she'd walked into the shed on the Davis land, thinking to confront Malcolm about the trap she'd found on her land. She hadn't seen him that day, and her welcome had been anything but friendly. It wasn't her fault the trucking section of the land was vast and had so many buildings. She never knew where the main office was located. Well, hell, she hadn't been on her uncle's turf since she'd been a teen and they'd had a family summer get-together. Better days, for sure.

She'd seen things a few days ago after wandering into the wrong building. And she suspected Malcolm knew that.

"I tried to find you the other day," she said, stepping back a bit. He used their proximity to his advantage, and she wasn't going to allow it. Shoving her fingers in her front pockets, she jutted out her elbows, enlarging her personal space. "I stopped by the place."

"I was told that. Reggie found you wandering around snooping."

"Nope. Wasn't snooping. I went there with a purpose. But that maze of buildings and parked trucks you've got over there will disorient anyone. I was looking for you, and I wasn't sure where the office was located. And I wasn't greeted very nicely, either."

"Reggie keeps a tight hand on security around the place."

"Not tight enough to allow me to wander for ten minutes and get lost. I'd appreciate it if you'd let Reggie know that family does not care to have a .32 caliber pointed at her. Nor…" Was she going there? She had to know. "Nor does family appreciate being shot at from across the lake."

Malcolm lifted his chin, looking down at her with her father's blue eyes. "What did you come by for, Skylar?"

No reply to her accusation? Probably because it was true. Damn it!

He sucked in the corner of his lower lip, a weird habit she'd noticed he did often. That is, when she saw him. Skylar made a point of not associating with Malcolm's bunch. Much as her father had tried to be kind to his brother, they'd struggled to the end.

"I almost stepped into a snare trap placed on my property. Thought it was one of yours."

"And why would you think something like that?"

Beating about the bush regarding the situation was not endearing him to her. And the hairs on the back of her neck were prickling more intensely the longer he studied her.

"Because I know you and your employees have a nasty habit of poaching. Cole told me."

"Did he?" Another suck at his lip. "Cole Pruitt. You know when I told you I'd hired him part-time, I hadn't expected you to break it off with him. You lost yourself a good one there, Skylar."

"If that's what you consider good, then I have to question your moral leanings."

"You've got that high-and-mighty streak like your father had, Skylar. It's not appealing."

"I'm not trying to appeal to you, other than to ask that you'll respect the property borders and not set traps on my land. I do a lot of hiking through the woods. My father made a point of ensuring the trails and off trails were safe."

"About that land…" Malcolm glanced over her shoulder, squinting at the sunlight. "You know my offer to buy that north parcel still stands. But not for much longer."

Skylar tilted her head. "I'm still considering it."

Was she? Dad wouldn't have wanted her to sell.

"It's just a quarter-mile section on the north end, Skylar."

"You've already got an access road to the highway."

"But cutting across through the end of my brother's land would reduce travel times measurably."

"It's my land now."

"What happens if you die?"

Skylar's jaw dropped open and she quickly snapped it shut. The audacity of such a terrible question should not surprise her, coming from her uncle, but it did.

"Someone shot at me last night, Malcolm. Nearly missed boring a hole right through my brain. So I almost did die."

Malcolm was too fidgety right now, and he'd stopped sucking on his lip.

"That's a shame. It really is. But what about that shelter I understand you want to build? Some sort of wildlife sanctuary?" he asked.

The only one who could have told him about that was Cole. He had not been involved with Malcolm when they'd first started dating. Skylar wasn't sure at what point they'd hooked up and Cole had started doing things for him. Illegal things. And he'd been drinking, too. He'd never been a drinker before.

"Cole told me you'd lost your cosigner for the loan," Malcolm said.

Because Cole had been going to cosign on the half-million-dollar loan. It would take a frosty day in July now for Skylar to ever trust that man again.

"That's none of your concern," she said.

"It could be," he said quickly. "You sell me that land and I'll cosign for you. I'll go you one better, and put down earnest money that I'm sure you'll need."

The offer was not what she should want. But a flat-out refusal stuck in her throat and she had to swallow to keep from swearing at him. It was all that she wanted. A means to begin her dream.

"Think about it," he said. "And do be careful, Skylar. Calling the police on your family is unkind."

"I didn't—"

He sucked in his lip loudly.

"Only a fool *wouldn't* call the police after nearly being shot," she said.

"And you are certainly no fool."

"Never have been, never will be." She had to hold back a wince, because she had been a fool in a wedding dress two months earlier. And he knew it. "We done here?"

Malcolm nodded.

Skylar had to walk around him to get to the driver's side of her truck. He didn't move, just watched her slide in behind the wheel, and when she was ready to back up, he still stood there, eyeing her in the side mirror. It was a cool yet malicious look, and it prickled her skin. He was not a man to mess with. As her father had well known.

And he had just given her another warning.

After shifting into Reverse, she waited as he slowly turned and walked away, straight behind her truck, which meant she wasn't able to leave until she could see that he was halfway across the lot.

"Bastard," she muttered.

She couldn't help but think her dad would want her to build the shelter. She'd told him about her dreams for it. He'd said she must do it.

But to surrender some of the land to do so?

She had to say no to Malcolm. Her dreams would be dashed, but at least she'd remain true to her dad.

Chapter Six

Joe watched Lucy Carnet, the forensic lab tech, work meticulously over the snare trap Brent had brought in earlier. He didn't often show up to wait for results, but today his focus had narrowed solely on this investigation. Because Skylar could have been hurt, or worse.

No more dallying with the poachers. He would track them down. And if they had been the ones to shoot at Skylar, a conviction would be secured.

The lab was a mobile van that traveled the county. Most forensic work could be done in this lab; they covered everything from bodily fluid identification to explosives and firearms examination.

"Any DNA?" Joe asked after about twenty minutes of watching Lucy pluck out bits of grass and other minutiae from the steel cable.

"Dude, I won't have that answer until I've examined these specimens. Could take a few hours or even a few days, because I still have to send it in to the crime lab in Duluth for analysis. Sorry."

"Right. I knew that. But the shell casings are definitely manufactured by Lapua."

Lucy had looked at those first and had, surprisingly, guessed the make because they were similar to a recent bullet casing she'd studied.

"I'd say so. Was an easy match. Italian-made bullets, which are often used with the Finnish-made sniper rifle by the same name. Surprisingly common in this county."

A sniper rifle was serious business. And it made the hairs on Joe's arms prickle to know someone had Skylar in his sights. Had a professional shot at her? Joe had to wonder who had such skill to sight in a target at that distance. And come close enough to merely deliver a warning skim across her ear and not accidentally kill her. Could the shooter be ex-military, like his brother Jason?

"You going to check the local gun registry?" Lucy asked.

"Of course, but I suspect we won't find any matches."

"You never know. There are all sorts of guns all over the state. Heard your brother was involved in a gunrunning investigation in Duluth."

"Jason?" Joe shrugged. "He had a close encounter with the Minnesota mafia and a related foreign contact, but no guns were seized. It was a murder investigation, actually."

And Jason did like to brag about that case to Joe and their older brother, Justin. It had been a coup for Jason after he'd been removed from his CIA duty and placed in the small town of Frost Falls as their chief of police. A town of less than a thousand people, where the most interesting law enforcement activity involved an old man who liked to walk naked down Main Street whenever he got toasted. Which, according to his brother's wincing recounts, was often.

As a result of the murder investigation, Jason had hooked up with a pretty French Interpol agent who was still hanging around. Good for him. Joe suspected Jason would pop the question soon. They had plans to move to Ely, since Jason was considering taking a position with the county law enforcement, and his girlfriend had been selling her nature photographs at local events and doing quite well.

But Joe always picked up on his big brothers' subtle digs that Joe was just a fish and game officer who saw no real action. Despite his law enforcement training, he was a peace officer, with a further two-year degree in wildlife management. Joe just caught fishermen without licenses and talked to the trees and wolves, they said.

They would never know how much those teasing words—that he was a nature boy and was comfortable with his place in this world, and how it coincided with all things wild, wooly and winged—dug into Joe's soul. But his job was more than mere lake patrol and babysitting the trees. He not only protected the wildlife but the humans, as well. He may not be cruising the alleys looking for drug dealers or busting child trafficking rings, but he made a difference in a part of the world that needed protection and understanding. And this poaching investigation would hopefully not only cease the poaching of wolves and their dwindling population, but also lead him to Max's killer.

Max had to have stepped on someone's toes. He would never purposely approach a poacher. Max had been nonviolent and believed that those who did wrong would answer to their greater power. But might he accidentally have stumbled upon some poachers? Seen something he shouldn't have?

Just like Joe suspected Skylar had. What had she seen—or what did she know—that someone needed to threaten her to keep silent about?

"Dude, do not lean on the exam table."

Joe straightened and lifted the heel of his palm from the steel table near the lab tech's elbow. "Sorry. I was thinking."

"Difficult to do more than two things at once? I get it."

"You are an annoying white coat," Joe jested, because he knew the lab techs hated that term.

"Touché. Now I'm going to run some boring machines for a few hours so…"

"I'm going to have a look at the gun registry," he told Lucy. "Call me as soon as you've got anything."

"Will do, Cash."

Joe left the van and wandered outside, where he inhaled the fresh air through his nose and pulled it deep into his lungs. So his job offered plenty of sunshine, clean air and outdoor activity. What was wrong with that? Nothing at all.

But he would show his brothers that he wasn't merely a nature boy. And he sensed Skylar had suddenly become the key to achieving that goal.

THE CAT HAD been beyond hope by the time Skylar arrived. There wasn't a rib that hadn't been broken, and she suspected a crushed skull, as well. Its breathing had been so slow, and five minutes after she'd arrived the cat had passed away. Poor kitty. She wouldn't have had much chance for survival even if Skylar had taken her home with her. She was in a better place now.

Skylar gave Becky a kiss on her bald head and set her on the ground. It had taken no more than forty-five minutes to knit a tiny sweater that slipped over her body. The red color really worked on her. She loved to scamper about, showing the other animals her new duds. She'd been born featherless—save the one straight white tail feather—and needed that extra coat to stay warm, even in the summer. Also, the sweater protected her from mosquitos and sunburn.

The purpose of a breed of featherless chicken that had been bred in a lab? To provide for easier and more efficient handling in factory farms. Skylar thought it inhumane, and just another means of man trying to play God. She was not a vegetarian, but when she did eat chicken, it was always one she had butchered herself. It wasn't right to eat something that had been tortured for the plate.

Becky was an anomaly, born of two feathered chickens. Her human owners, who lived on the farm just south of the Davis land, had almost killed her, but then had asked Skylar if she'd be interested in caring for her. Skylar had jumped at the opportunity. Just because an animal had been born different didn't mean it did not deserve a chance.

As for Stella, she had been born with four legs and had been a member of a pack, and, once again, man's cruelty had irrevocably altered an animal's life. She traveled well on three legs, but the loss of her pack had left her half the wolf she could have been. She remained cheerful and always by Skylar's side, but there seemed to be days the wolf moped. Skylar felt sure, when the distant howl of a wolf sounded on a clear night, that the look on Stella's face was sadness.

You could take the animal out of the wild, but you could never take the wild out of the animal. Still, Skylar had known that to even try to force Stella back into her pack would have resulted in her being ostracized, possibly even killed. She was marked by humans now.

Pulling a rawhide strip out of her back pocket, Skylar waggled it before the wolf, who, rather than moping, was rather curiously watching as Becky strutted off to show the others her new sweater.

"Treat?" Skylar asked.

Stella pawed the ground and sat. Skylar had not taught her that; she was simply a polite wolf.

She handed over the strip and ruffled Stella's fur behind her ear, where she loved a good scratch. "Have at it, sweetie. I'm going around back to keep an eye on the fire."

She'd lit the bonfire again this afternoon, and this time had poked the remains of her wedding dress farther into the stone circle. The flames were low, but the snaps and crackles lured Skylar closer. Sweet, smoky perfume curled enticingly about her. A few inches of hem remained on the dress. She grabbed the fire-poking stick and stabbed at the fabric, consigning the last traces of her stupidity to the flames.

Joe hadn't asked about the dress, but he had seen it. And if he was investigating poaching in the area, Skylar figured one of their future conversations might veer back around to the damned dress. It was inevitable. Because the information she had about Cole Pruitt placed him suspiciously in the poaching camp. She didn't want to go there with Joe, but how not to?

The trees on the distant shore across the lake were a deep green line, capped by softer jagged green, where they segued into the graying sky. Looked like rain. She loved the rain, especially sitting out on the deck and watching it scatter on the lake. Rain would keep poachers out of the woods.

And, hopefully, snipers.

Shrugging a hand up her opposite arm, she squinted to focus on where Joe had pointed when he'd been guessing the shooter's position. How long had the shooter stood there, sighting her in, waiting for the perfect moment to pull the trigger? And had it been merely a warning? Or had the shooter missed the target? *Her.*

Malcolm had avoided answering when she'd asked him about it.

Exhaling heavily through her nose, she shook her head. She'd done nothing to deserve such treatment. Even dumping an ex-boyfriend who thought he could tell her what to do, when to do it and how to do it didn't warrant being sniped at.

"Cole," she muttered. "I sure as hell hope you're not involved in this."

As Joe pulled up the driveway to his home, he received a call from Lucy. She'd gotten a DNA match from the snare. And it was startling.

Joe left his coat on a hook inside the foyer and wandered into the cool one-story house set at the corner of a tidy block in Checker Hill. He'd moved to the next town over from his parents' farm after his brother Justin had suggested the town had some nice real estate at good prices. Jason lived forty-five minutes away in Frost Falls. All the Cash boys lived in or around the Boundary Waters.

He would much prefer to live out in the country, and was working toward that goal. His savings were stacking up, and he kept an eye on the DNR land-release posts. Every so often they put up a parcel of land for sale, though it wasn't usually zoned for building. More often it was sold as hunting land, but with work, any chunk of forested land could be made livable. A real home smack in the middle of the nature he thrived upon.

He pushed the button on the coffee maker and placed a mug under it. He tugged off his work shirt and tossed it over the back of a kitchen chair. He hadn't gone out on the lake today, instead spending most of the day in the forensic lab and behind his desk checking databases. He did not go into an office each day. He had an office here at home. Most conservation officers worked out of their homes. He reported to the district lieutenant, who also made his schedule and assigned territories. Throw in a county-issued four-by-four truck, boat and Jet Ski?

He felt sure his brothers would never admit their envy of that sweet arrangement.

What he needed was a shower and a good workout session to stretch out the kinks from sleeping in the car all night. Surveilling, that was. Keeping an eye out for Skylar. Because if he couldn't be near her, at the very least he could ensure her safety.

A call to Skylar was due. He needed to ask her a few more questions, because the DNA taken from the snare had turned up something too interesting to ignore. The shell casings had been clean. Joe suspected they may or may not have been touched by the same person who set the snare. Yet they definitely matched the Lapua rifle, and if they ever found another spent casing or bullet, that same rifle would leave familiar etchings, much like a fingerprint. So that was a positive.

But the better lead had been the DNA. There had been a hair entwined in the snare that the lab had gotten a clean read off. And that hair had matched a person already on record in the database due to a few minor infractions a couple years ago. One bar fight that had resulted in busted ribs to the other guy and an assault charge. DNA extraction was now standard procedure during a booking if the offense the person was charged for could include jail time.

Joe was thankful whenever a match showed up because that made his job easier.

But this time around? Following up on this lead was going to try his soul. He hadn't seen his former best friend, Cole Pruitt, for over a year. Because he hadn't wanted to look in the man's eyes and know he had been the one to win Skylar.

Now, he'd look in those eyes and decide whether Cole was capable of shooting at Skylar. Or, worse, poisoning an old man.

Chapter Seven

Joe wandered across the front lawn before the house he knew belonged to Cole Pruitt. Or, at least, it had a year ago. Now the little two-bedroom rambler had a for-sale sign stuck in the overgrown lawn. A faded garden gnome with a broken red cap lay on its back in a patch of clover—a victim of neighborhood vandals, surely. A peek through the front window showed bare walls, hardwood floors and no sign of life inside.

When he'd decided not to pay attention to Cole and Skylar after they'd hooked up, Joe had no idea Cole would literally slip off his radar. Had he moved elsewhere in town? This town boasted four thousand people. Not small, and not large, either. Most people knew the majority of the citizens, and neighbors always looked after one another.

Speaking of which, the neighbor drove his Honda up the driveway next door. Joe waved and walked across the lawn, signaling for the driver to roll down his window, which he did.

"I'm looking for Cole Pruitt," Joe said. He was in

uniform, so it wouldn't seem odd to a stranger that he was asking.

"Haven't seen that fellow in a couple months. Thought he was getting married. Must have packed up the wife and moved on," the man said. "Is there a problem, Officer?"

"No. Just checking in on an old friend. I've lost track of him over the last year."

The man shrugged. "Then you know him better than I do. He was never around much, and I didn't have a chance to get to know him because up until recently I've been working the night shift."

"You said he had a wife?"

"Oh, I don't know. I did see a woman going in once in a while. Just assumed. Like I said, didn't pay much attention to him. You might try his parents?"

Cole's parents lived a few miles out of town on a small alpaca ranch. "Thanks. Good idea. Have a great day."

Joe walked back to his vehicle and slid inside. He picked up the forensic report that detailed Cole Pruitt's DNA being found in the snare trap. That land where he'd found the snare must edge up against Skylar's land. Or could it belong to Davis Trucking? He knew the Davis families owned land plots next to one another. He'd have to take out a map and get a handle on the area. Maybe Cole had set the snare, thinking it was on Skylar's land? Which would then make Joe suspect Skylar had knowledge of that.

A wife? Joe's thoughts went to that burned wedding dress in the smoldering firepit.

Why wasn't Skylar being completely honest with him?

His heart sank to think of the possibility that she could be involved in the poaching he'd been trying to pin on the Davis family.

Malcolm Davis *was* her uncle. That family's tendency toward criminal activity was well-known in the area. Yet they covered their tracks well. Misdemeanors and the occasional overweight truckload were all that local law enforcement had ever been able to charge them with. Joe had to wonder if someone on his side of the law was helping Davis. Was a dirty cop in their midst? It wasn't out of the realm of possibility.

Just like it was possible that Skylar Davis could be working for her uncle.

Did Joe know her as well as he thought he did?

WIELDING IN ONE hand a wooden spoon dripping tomato sauce, Skylar opened the front door with her other, fully expecting the man standing there with his hands stuffed in his front pants pockets. Or rather, hoping it would be him.

"Joe. Just in time."

He checked over his shoulder, then quirked his brow at her. "I am?"

She licked the spoon. Hmm, it needed a touch more garlic. "I'm making supper. I always make too much pasta. Want to join me?"

"That's a no-brainer." He stepped inside and closed the door behind him.

Skylar sailed into the kitchen in time to turn off the stove buzzer that announced her roasted garlic was done. She took the small terra-cotta crock out from the oven and opened the lid. Inside, the garlic bulb had shriveled and browned, and smelled sweetly delicious.

Stella poked her nose against the patio screen door, and when she spied Joe her tail began to wag.

"Hey, Stella, good to see you again. Does she stay outside?"

"No, you can let her in. She'll want to taste the pasta, too."

He opened the screen door, knelt before the wolf, who stood as high as his head, and received a tongue lash across his jaw and hair.

It warmed Skylar's heart to see the two interact. Cole had always been afraid of the wolf and had shown it by trying to be the alpha, always ordering Stella to go lie down or go outside "where the wild things belong." Stella had not liked him, often showing her teeth and growling at him, but she'd never attacked, though Skylar feared she was capable of doing just that. Strangely, the wolf had tried to appeal to the obnoxious male by following him around, and once she'd even sat close to him outside on the deck—bless her loving but misdirected heart. She was as poor as Skylar at recognizing a good man.

"So did you stop by for a free meal or police business?" Skylar asked as she set another plate on the counter that stretched along the kitchen and served as the divider between it and the living area.

"Both?" Joe's smile was the sexiest thing this side of the Boundary Waters. "I got lucky with the meal. No man will ever turn down a home-cooked meal. It's in our genes to say yes to these things."

"Yeah? What if it's tofu on the menu?"

"Yes, yes and yes."

Skylar smirked. She remembered the one time she'd wanted him to say yes, and he had not. Her jaw tensed.

Realizing she was standing there thinking too hard, Skylar had to catch a drip that fell from the spoon before it landed on the floor. The man had to be aware of his stunning toothpaste-commercial smile and the effect it had on women. And combine that with the dark hair and stubble—devastatingly sexy. How to remain the strong, independent woman that she strove to be when all she wanted to do was snuggle up against him and see what developed between the two of them?

"I got some answers from the forensic lab this afternoon," he said as he slid onto a stool in front of the counter.

"You know who was shooting at me?"

"No. The lab is still running a trace on the shell casings to see it they match any recent findings. But I did get an ID on the make and model. They're from a foreign weapon. Italian-made."

"That's interesting. And weird. Is there a strange Italian wandering around the lake, taking shots at me?"

His chuckle didn't sound at all mirthful. "It was used in the Gulf War, which makes it a popular sell for gun enthusiasts here in the States. It's a sniper rifle. Whoever took that shot had to be a pro."

"Like a professional sniper? That's pretty far-fetched, don't you think?"

"Sharpshooting is a hobby and a profession. As well, there could be any number of ex-military personnel living in the area who may have specialized in sniping. My brother was a sniper."

"That's right. He's up in Frost Falls, isn't he?"

"You keep track of our family?"

"Hard not to with the annual charity calendar. You made a great Mr. February, by the way."

Did the man actually blush? Oh, sweet mercy. Skylar was in trouble with this one. She pulled a bottle of craft beer brewed by her favorite Minneapolis brewery from the fridge and handed it to him.

"Thanks." He screwed off the cap and tilted back a swallow. "I'm off duty, so I don't mind having a beer. But I do have some questions for you."

"Can they wait until after I've plied you with my famous tomato sauce?"

"Of course. I don't know that I've been plied before."

She smirked. "Stella and I will do our best."

With that, Joe winked at Stella, and the wolf eagerly wagged her tail. She had fallen for the guy, the poor girl. Was Skylar next in line?

THE MEAL WAS SUBLIME. And sitting next to Joe at the counter, sharing conversation, a couple cold double IPAs, and the creamy tomato sauce and pasta, Skylar had a stunning realization. She missed sharing meals with another person. And not just with her favorite wolf.

Or maybe it was that for the first time, she really enjoyed this man's company and couldn't imagine not enjoying it all the time. That threw her off course a little. Since when did she want a man around?

When Joe prompted her for possibly the second time, she startled. "Huh? Oh, sorry. Was just thinking."

"You've been distracted since I arrived. You okay, Skylar? How's your ear?"

Touching the tip of her ear, she glanced his way, then quickly averted her gaze. Due to their proximity, her body hummed with desire. Yes, she was distracted. By everything Joe Cash. It wasn't right. Was it? It could be. But no. He said he was here to ask her questions about the investigation. And she would be a fool to believe anything else could happen beyond polite police-citizen interaction.

"It's fine," she finally said. "Just a bruise, really. And I'm always okay." Because she could never admit when she was not. "You said you wanted to ask me stuff." She pushed her plate forward and leaned her elbows on the counter. "I still have no idea who could have shot at me. And now that you think it's a sniper...?" She shook her head, at a loss.

"I believe you. Do you have a map of your property and the surrounding area? I'm not sure if I was on DNR land last night when I found the snare. I know the property lines around here snake a lot."

"They do, and there are weird little arms that jut out from my land here and there that sort of mesh together like a puzzle piece with Malcolm's property. But there's also some DNR land around the lake. I have a map. It's in the office. Do you want me to get it right now?"

"Would you? I was going to look it up on the county registry, but my laptop has been recharging out in the truck since I had that idea."

"No problem. Give me a few minutes. Stella, keep an eye on Joe."

She left them and veered down the hallway to the office, which was next to her bedroom. It was a relief to take a breather from sitting so close to the guy. But she wouldn't be so blatant as Stella, positioning herself right beside his chair and eyeing him constantly with tongue lolling out.

This had been her dad's office, and it was still furnished in dark brown leather, green-and-blue flannel curtains, and the enlarged photographs of insects he'd taken while on his daily hikes. She loved the dragonfly print, and felt sure the critter was smiling each time she looked at its big alien mug.

On the top shelf in the closet, she found the rolled map that her dad had given her just a month before his death. The lawyer held all the property papers and title. She hadn't had a chance to get her hands on those, and hadn't felt a need since losing the last good man she'd had in her life.

She clutched the map to her chest. It had been a sad day when he'd handed her this. Her dad had insisted she sit down and plan his funeral right then and there. He'd listed the songs he wanted sung and the bible verses spoken. It had torn Skylar's heart from her chest, but she had maintained a stiff visage and had gotten through it. Only later, when she'd found a few moments to walk along the lakeshore by herself, had she succumbed to wailing tears. No one should ever have to plan a funeral with the person for whom that solemn affair was to honor.

That first year after her father's death had been difficult. If she hadn't had Stella to hold and hug and cry to, Skylar wasn't sure she would have made it through at all. It wasn't as if she had a mother to hold her and tell her everything was going to be all right. She often wondered if Dorothy Davis was even aware of her husband's death. They'd never officially divorced following her mother literally fleeing the family. And when Skylar had asked her dad if he'd wanted her to find her mom to notify her of things, he'd simply shaken his head.

The past few years had tried her, yet Skylar was a survivor. She proudly stood upon the land her father had cherished as if it were a part of his very being. Because she knew exactly what it had meant to him. She'd grown up on this land, and felt as though the lake ran in her veins and the earth formed her bones. She had, as the best memories from summers, racing through the woods with a pet fox or climbing oak trees and hanging upside down from a maple branch with bent legs. Or swimming in the lake and diving for turtles nestled in the mud.

Skylar couldn't imagine living anywhere else in the world. This was home, where her roots had burrowed deep into the soil. And nothing could uproot her.

But was she safe now?

With the rolled map tucked under an arm, she wandered out to the kitchen to find Joe rinsing the dishes and placing them in the dishwasher.

"Oh, I can do that."

"No, problem," he said. "It's the least I can do for the free meal. See what your plying did to me?"

"I'll have to ply you more often." She set the map on the clean counter and rolled it open. "This is the detailed map of the Davis property—my property—and its boundaries. And this other one looks like the entire county." She pulled that map on top and perused it. Joe joined her on the opposite side of the counter. She pointed out her land on the bigger map of the county. "I'm here."

He turned the map around and studied it. "So I was right. That's DNR land across the lake. And looks like you're hugged on two sides by privately owned land for about three-quarters of your property."

"Right. The top part of it, which hugs the Boundary Waters, is not usable land. It's thick forest up there."

"But you're paralleled by two different land owners. Who owns this plot?"

"The Enersons," she said. "They're in their nineties. They've owned that land longer than my family has had this land. They don't have any children. I imagine their land will be auctioned off when they die. I should really save for that, but all my funds are going to my dream cache."

"Your dream cache?"

"The shelter I want to build."

"Oh, right. You'll do it. I know you will."

"I appreciate the confidence."

"What about these plots?" Joe pointed out the three plots that hugged her property on the west side.

"All three parcels are owned by the same person. That's an old access road," she said when Joe ran his finger along a red line that crossed over the very tip of her property. "I check the fence once a month. In the winter the snowmobiles try to plow through, and in the summer, I find truck tracks through there. I shouldn't mind, but it is my property and I do have it fenced."

"So the only way from this side of the lake to the other is to use this access road?" Joe asked.

"Or go the long way around. The only people who would need to use the access road would be people in a hurry."

"Who owns those three parcels?" he asked.

Skylar swallowed, then quickly said, "Malcolm Davis."

He met her gaze, and she knew what he was thinking. Most were aware of the trouble between the two Davis brothers. And since the townspeople were in the know, they knew to walk a wide circle around Malcolm Davis.

"Your uncle." He tapped the map. "The two of you… get along?"

The question felt heavy in her throat. An expected question from a police officer, especially a conservation officer, and she wasn't sure how to answer. Not this time.

"We don't invite each other to tea parties. Why do you ask?"

Joe shrugged. "I know there was some kind of family feud. I need to ask all the questions, Skylar."

"I understand. No, we're not friendly. I keep my distance and so does he." Except when she'd gone to talk to him. "Malcolm wants to buy some of my land."

"You going to sell?"

"It would help fund my dream cache. But my dad would never sell. That was the reason for their feud, among other things." Skylar had never gotten the details, but she suspected it had something to do with her mother and her alliance to the wrong brother. "So I'm struggling between keeping it for my dad's sake and selling it for the animals I could help."

"Tough decision."

"It is."

"Would your uncle stoop to threatening you, trying to coerce you to sell?"

"Oh, I don't think so." But as for keeping quiet about whatever she'd seen? With a confession on her tongue, Skylar was cut off by Joe's next move.

He pressed the heels of his palms to the counter and leaned forward, making direct eye contact with her. "Skylar, what's up with you and Cole Pruitt?"

She sucked in her lower lip. Now that was a question she wasn't prepared to answer.

Chapter Eight

"There's nothing up," Skylar said.

Feeling the need for distance from Joe's probing gaze, she pulled open the screen door and stepped onto the deck. Joe followed close on her heels. When she propped her elbows on the deck railing and looked down over the fire pit, the ashes showing no sign of white satin and pearls and lace, she breathed in the lingering scent of smoke and soot. The perfume of regret.

Joe put his elbows on the railing a foot away from her. Maybe she shouldn't have been so eager to invite him in for supper. Now she'd have to face some truths about her own miserable sense of want and trust issues.

Joe rubbed his jaw, taking in the evening quiet. The lake glittered and crickets chirped. The evening smelled liquid and green. When his gaze dropped downward, he asked, "Why was the wedding dress in the fire?"

Skylar straightened, gripping the railing with both hands. "I was taking care of something I should have done months ago. We didn't get married, Joe. And I don't want to talk about it other than to say I learned Cole wasn't the man I thought he was."

"I'm sorry."

"You and Cole used to be good friends," she prompted. "He'd talk about you."

"Yeah, well, I tried to avoid him after…"

"After?"

He shrugged. "He hooked up with you. Didn't want to stand in the way."

"You didn't think you could still be Cole's and my friend because we were dating?"

He smirked and shook his head. "Not really. Skylar, you were…are…" He huffed out a breath. "Screw it. I'm just going to put this out there, then you'll know."

Skylar turned to him, knowing what was coming. Because she felt the same? No, because Joe wore his heart on his sleeve, and that was one fine garment.

"I like you, Skylar. Have been attracted to you for a long time. You know that."

"I do. Or I did."

"I know our timing never seemed to work out. You were always seeing someone, or I was."

"Or you were refusing my proposition," she added quickly, then winced. Not the time for that one.

He turned, and eyed her steadily. "Are you still hung up on that night of the wedding, Skylar?"

She looked aside. *Petty* and *stupid* were two things that came to mind.

"If I could change that night, I would," he said. "We were both drunk. There was no way I was going to have sex with you—with any woman—when she wasn't clear in her head. That's just wrong. Though I sure wish you would have made that offer when we were sober."

She did, as well. Yes, he had done the right thing, but her needy self, desperate for attention from the right man, had taken it as an affront.

Time to move beyond that. Life had changed. She had changed. Mostly. Apparently, she was still trying to figure men out.

"I thought you avoided me after that because I'd said something wrong," she managed. "It shouldn't matter anymore. It doesn't."

"No, it doesn't. Because two weeks after that party you and Cole hooked up. When the two of you got together?" He bowed his head and didn't say anything else. His whole body sank, shoulders bowing forward as he adjusted his weight against the railing.

He didn't need to say more. Skylar had felt the same sort of letdown. She'd chosen Cole over Joe. A man who had never measured up to Joe Cash. Quiet, gentle Joe with a good heart and, as she well knew, who possessed a well-honed physique from sparring at the gym. His physicality was the yang to his mental and emotional yin. She sensed he needed that physical punishment to his body to counter the softness within that strove to always do right.

And she'd known at the time what had occurred between the two men because she had chosen one over the other. Skylar had sensed, after a month or two of dating Cole, and not seeing Joe anymore, that Joe had tucked his head under like a scolded pup and hadn't wanted to deal with her or the idea that they hadn't worked out. And she'd blamed him for that drunken night fiasco when she should have let it go.

Cole had pursued her aggressively, and she'd fallen into his forceful charm. It had been a weird, false sense of security she'd felt when she was with him. He'd bought her things, told her she was beautiful and was always texting her innuendoes. To think on it now, it had been like a high school crush—the jock deeming to date the nerdy girl. A facade of desperation she hadn't seen through until it was too late and she'd donned white satin and lace.

Thank goodness she had learned his truth. Through Malcolm Davis, of all people.

"I haven't talked to him for a couple months. Cole's been living off-the-grid," she offered. Joe lifted his head, curious now. "I believe he's trying to sell his house in town."

"I stopped by to talk to him. It's listed with a realtor. Empty inside. Where did he go?"

"He's...north somewhere." She waved her hand in that direction, unable to summon curiosity to the man's whereabouts. "Still comes in to Checker Hill once in a while to pick up groceries and stuff." She had seen his truck but always turned the opposite direction to avoid actually making eye contact. "My guess is you'll find him most often on Lake Seraphim. He likes to fish and...that's all I know about the guy, Joe. Can we leave it at that?"

He nodded. "I need to find him. Ask him about the snare trap Officer Kofax almost stepped in while we were searching across the lake. Did you know Cole was poaching in the area?"

She nodded vaguely. She knew things about Cole.

About Malcolm Davis and his crew. And…a glance to the hitching post with the bullet holes in it silenced her.

"Really?" Joe noticed her focus. "Don't let anyone tell you what to do, Skylar. You know I've got your back, don't you?"

"You do?" Speaking the words loosened something in her throat, and she sensed if she didn't lift her chin a tear would also threaten. "Why? Why do I matter to you?"

"Skylar, you shouldn't even have to ask that."

No, she knew the answer. Joe cared about most everyone. And she had known she had broken his heart by choosing Cole.

"If someone is threatening you or holding something over on you," he said, "you know you can trust me enough to tell me."

"Thanks, Joe, but right now I've got to trust myself and sort things out alone regarding Cole Pruitt. The burned dress was a beginning. I'm trying to stand on my own and be independent."

"You've always been independent. That's the reason we never—" He cleared his throat. "Right. Whatever you need to do. But just so you know, I'm not stopping until I learn who took a shot at you."

"I can take care of myself, Joe."

"Still not changing my mind about protecting you."

She put her palm on her forehead.

"You're stuck with me. Like it or not," he added firmly.

And all Skylar could do was smile a little. Because much as she wanted to push him away, she needed to pull him closer. She suspected he knew that and had probably known that far longer than she had. The man had been a part of her life for a long time. Why was she only now realizing just how important that part had been to her? He was like an anchoring post in a building she wished to erect. That shelter could not function without him.

Ah, hell. She'd made a huge mistake by getting engaged to Cole Pruitt. Much bigger than she'd realized.

Joe straightened to leave, but then leaned against the railing, his hands gripping the wood. "This is the wrong time to ask, but—"

"Ask," she said in a rush before she realized how desperate she sounded. "I mean, I think I know what you're going to ask about, and it's okay, Joe. *We're* okay. I've made some wrong choices in my life. But knowing you has never been wrong. I hope we can—"

He moved swiftly, dipping his head and meeting her mouth with his. It was a surprise kiss, but one that made her sigh all over. His hair dusted her brow, tickling it. The masculine warmth of him drew her closer, their bodies conforming. The stubble on his cheek glided under her fingertips as she stroked down his jaw and clung to his shirt to keep him close. Her breath caught.

Overwhelmed by him, yet not wanting to lose the heady feeling of lightness that swept over her, she tilted onto her tiptoes and deepened the kiss. She'd been kissed by many, but never had she lost herself so quickly and so freely as right now. The world slipped away.

When he pulled back, a small smile curled his mouth. "Had to do that."

"It was a long time coming," Skylar said.

Joe smiled more widely. "That answered a lot of questions."

"I'm glad that was how you chose to ask them."

"I'd better get going. Got some paperwork to do. Can I check in with you tomorrow?"

"I'll be here." She tapped her lips. "Waiting for another kiss."

He nodded and then wandered down the stairs to the ground and around the side of the cabin. Stella glanced to Skylar. *Should I follow him?* she seemed to ask.

Skylar patted her thigh, and the wolf skipped up the steps to her side. She wanted to race around the cabin and follow Joe to his truck, jump into his arms and kiss him deeply and for as long as she could, until her breath got lost in him.

But she stopped that impulsive need for connection with a man she hadn't realized she'd wanted so much until now.

LUCY HAD RECORDED her findings on the state database that went directly to the Bureau of Criminal Apprehension located in Saint Paul. Joe was on the phone with Harvey Logan, a BCA officer who had cross-referenced the data from the rifle shell casings and the bullet to other evidence collected from crime scenes across the state, as well as the entire United States.

"No matches," Officer Logan said, after keeping Joe on hold five minutes. "Which only means that if the same rifle was used to commit a crime previously, we just didn't find the evidence."

"Right." Joe scribbled down the officer's name and thanked him. The BCA would come out, process and investigate crime scenes, if needed. He didn't feel he needed the help yet. "You ever work with the Fond du Lac police department out in Cloquet?"

"Sure. You think this is tribal related?"

"No. I don't know. I've got another investigation. Native American man died from poisoning a few weeks ago. Not sure if it's related, but feels as though it might be. I contacted the tribal police, but his death was ruled accidental so they are not investigating."

"Then why are you?"

"Like I said, just doesn't feel right. Thanks, Harvey. I may be checking in with you again, depending on what turns up."

"Always here. Call anytime."

Joe hung up, then tapped the eagle talon hanging from the leather cord at his neck. The day after Max's death, after he'd woken up in Max's campsite, Joe had headed to Max's home along with Brent Kofax. The small one-bedroom house sat on the Fond du Lac reservation. Max had suggested it wasn't really his home, for it closed him in when his soul wanted nothing more than air and earth and water surrounding him. The man had lived a remarkably minimalist life. Almost Zen, save for some photos and old glass Coke bottles he'd collected over the years.

No clues. No family, save for his tribe. On the mantle, Joe had studied a few black-and-white photos from powwows in which Max had once danced hoops decades earlier. His costume had been amazing, decorated with eagle feathers that Max had told Joe he'd collected since he was a boy, finding them in the forest, tucked here and there, and once he'd even found a dead eagle roadside, had said rites for it and then buried it.

Joe had yet to speak with anyone from Max's tribe. What could they say about him beyond that he was a lone wolf? On the other hand, someone had to have known him. Who took care of his home when he camped in the summer?

Now he rubbed his jaw as he searched the tribal records on the computer. He found a tribal elders list, and he thought one of the names sounded familiar. Had Max mentioned him over the years?

He picked up the phone, and when the call went to voice mail, he said, "This is Officer Joseph Cash with the DNR. I'm investigating the death of Max Owen and would like to talk to you about him. Please call me back." He left his phone number, then glanced to the bookshelf opposite his desk.

On the shelf above his books sat a few tokens he had collected over the years. A fist-sized chunk of agate he'd found on the shore of Lake Superior, nearly round thanks to millennia of churning in the waters. An iron cross his parents had given him on his confirmation day, forged from iron taken from local taconite mines. A wolf claw that he'd found in the forest as a teen. And… an eagle feather.

Joe got up and went over to the shelf. He picked up

the feather and turned it about. It was pure white, tipped with brown. The barbs were tight and the shaft strong.

What was it about eagles that seemed to gnaw at his instincts?

Chapter Nine

Joe navigated the boat along the southern edge of Lake Seraphim. The lake was shaped like an angel's wing, hence the name. He'd been told by a couple fishermen a quarter mile back that they'd seen Cole Pruitt cruise by and wave. This had always been his favorite spot for catching walleyes.

Joe had checked the fishing license database on his laptop. No current registry for Cole Pruitt. Nor was there a current address for Pruitt; it still listed the house in town that was for sale.

Spying the silver V-hull with the red blaze of flame across its stern, Joe moved in slowly, as he always did when approaching any fishermen in the area. He didn't want to scare off the fish or the people. And the DNR symbol emblazoned on the side of his boat let them know who he was. If someone were to suddenly fire up the engine and skid off, then he'd know something was up. He'd participated in a couple high-speed water chases in his service. He had to admit, the chase was a thrill.

He compared it to his brother Jason's love of snowmobiling. The guy should seriously consider professional racing. But Joe also added in Muay Thai fighting to get his physical adrenaline-rush thrills. He had to drive into Duluth to the gym to find opponents willing to match him, and when they did, the fight was on.

He used to spar with Cole. But that was then.

Pulling up alongside the boat, Joe waved to Cole, who nodded as he approached and put out his hand to catch the front of Joe's boat and steady it.

"Cash! I haven't seen you in a long time, buddy. Thought you were avoiding me for some strange reason."

Really? The man thought it was strange he'd avoid talking to a friend who had stolen the girl out from under him? Okay, that was unfair. He and Skylar had never officially dated.

"Been busy with work. I heard you were up this way so I wanted to talk to you. I have to do the official thing and ask to see your license."

Cole glanced to the cooler on the floor of the boat, which Joe guessed probably had a fish or five inside. The man had a fishing rod, not currently cast into the water, but it was propped aside the steering wheel, baited, and ready to cast. Near the driver's seat, a steel canteen wobbled on its side on the boat floor. It could contain anything from water to beer to—well, hell, Cole had never been much for hard liquor.

"You know walleyes are out of season right now?"

"Of course I do. Northerns and sturgeons right now. I'm sure I renewed my license this spring," Cole said. He made a show of patting his back pockets. "Never remember to carry my wallet with me from the car. Sorry, man. Just caught a few sunnies."

"Where are you parked?" Joe asked. The wake from a passing boat rocked his, and he gripped the edge of Cole's vessel tightly.

Cole nodded to the south. "Couple miles down. You going to make me go get my license to show you?"

Joe shook his head. "No, I trust you." He did not. And he knew the truth. But there was a bigger fish to fry this afternoon than an expired license. "There's actually a different reason I wanted to talk to you today."

"So this wasn't a coincidence, you running into me? Huh." The man crossed his arms over his chest. The wake wobbled them both, and Cole had to double step to keep his balance. In the process, he dipped forward too far. An odd move, Joe thought. "What's up? Still feeling sore over losing Skylar to me?"

The man's smirk had once made Joe laugh. They'd shared many a chuckle over beers and hockey games. Now it confused him.

"Doesn't appear as though you actually have her, does it?" Joe countered. Then he silently reprimanded himself for playing the one-up game. Skylar did not deserve such disrespect. "This isn't about Skylar. It's about the illegal snare trap I found across the lake from the Davis property."

Cole shrugged. "There are snares and traps all over the Superior Forest. It's what we hunters do. Oh, wait. I forgot. You're all into that save-the-wildlife thing. So what if I set a few traps?" A step backward had him losing his balance, and for the first time, Joe suspected Cole may have been drinking more than a beer or two.

"Depends on where and what you're hunting. Only thing in season right now is fish. And that snare looked like something set for a wolf."

"Thought it was illegal to trap wolves."

"It is." Joe lifted his jaw, meeting Cole's gaze defiantly. "A lab test found traces of your DNA on the snare. You set the trap, Cole. Which prompts my next question—just exactly what *are* you poaching and how long have you been doing it?"

Cole shook his head and chuckled. "Really? You're coming after me for that? Skylar told you, didn't she?"

"She didn't tell me anything. But it's true?"

"Did she tell you that I left her at the altar?"

"What?" Joe's jaw dropped open, but he caught himself and clamped his mouth shut. His fist curled as tight as his mouth.

"Yeah, she's a case, man. I couldn't go through with it. She was the one who talked me into doing some trapping for Malcolm. Oh. Oops." Cole's smirk had become obvious. Joe sensed he was either lying or, at the very least, stretching some weird truth. "Ah, hell, you're with fish and game. You know that family is dirty as crap. *All* of the Davis clan is. Including Skylar."

"Skylar would never—"

"They've been using her land. She hasn't said a word to anyone. Silence is the biggest yes in the world."

Resisting the urge to lash out at the man with a fist, Joe leaned forward, latching both hands onto the starboard side of Cole's boat. "You want me to believe Skylar forced you to set that trap?"

Cole shook his head. He swayed suddenly, and Joe caught a whiff of his breath. The scent was stronger than beer. "Nope. But she did get me involved with the family. She's not all innocent and as save-the-animals as you believe, man. That woman wants things. And she'll do what she needs to get 'em."

"What sort of things?"

Cole shrugged. "You know she's going to build some big old shed for broken-up animals. Wanted me to pay for it. Can you believe that?" he asked incredulously.

Joe did have a hard time believing Skylar would ask Cole for the money to build her shelter. That wouldn't make her much of an independent woman. On the other hand, he couldn't imagine how much a structure like that must cost. She might own a lot of land, but he'd never thought she was rich. Malcolm Davis, on the other hand, had money. And if Skylar were working for him…

"So what are you going to do?" Cole prompted. "Arrest me? Poaching is still a misdemeanor. I'll pay the fine right now. Only if you can show me the animal I snared."

"There was no animal in the snare." The police radio on the boat dashboard crackled with a call from Dispatch. Joe ignored it. "But we do have your DNA on the snare."

"Circumstantial evidence."

"You just admitted to poaching for the Davis family. I have a confession, yes?"

Cole shrugged.

"And you've been drinking."

"Oh, come on, man. Every fisherman out on a boat has a beer or two."

"You're not drinking beer. Smells like whiskey."

Cole waved a dismissive hand before him.

"Since when did you start drinking the hard stuff?"

"Since never!"

He was belligerent, and Joe was beginning to wonder if he was inebriated instead of merely tipsy. He stood well enough, his body only swaying with the wake of the boat.

Again the radio crackled, and this time Joe leaned over to grab the receiver. "What is it?"

"Got a crash on Lake Seraphim," Dispatch reported. "Jet Ski collided with a boat. Possible drowning. Isn't that where you said you were headed?"

"I'm here now. Send me the coordinates. I'll get there as quick as I can." Joe kicked against the side of Cole's boat to separate the vehicles. "You heard that."

"I did. Guess my ass is saved. For now."

"For now," Joe said curtly.

As he steered away from the smug idiot, Cole called, "She's not who you think she is!"

Tightening his jaw, Joe headed back in the direction he'd come.

Skylar was involved with Malcolm Davis? He didn't want to believe it. How could she possibly be? Cole had to be lying. It had been the booze talking. But *he* had left her at the altar? That was a good reason for a woman to burn her wedding dress. To dispose of bad memories.

And if a man like Cole Pruitt had deemed to leave

her at the altar, that really made Joe question Skylar's ethics. Was she putting up a front for him? Using the worthy cause of an animal shelter as a means to cover for her support of Davis's poaching habits?

Max had once said something about seeing into a person's soul, how sometimes their exterior acted counter to what the universe had initially sent them to do. Joe knew that. People smiled on the outside, while inside they could be smirking. But Skylar? Really?

The radio crackled again, and Joe answered that he was on his way. Local lifeguards would also be called, but if he got there first, he might have to go for a swim.

All in a day's work.

Skylar crumpled the refusal papers from the bank for the loan she'd signed for herself. She needed collateral. Dare she risk putting up the land? It had been sacred to her father, which was why she should never sell to Malcolm. Even if his offer to cosign felt like the rescue rope she needed right now.

Besides, she had a suspicion that Malcolm's need to buy the land was not altruistic. Sure, it would make the drive for his trucks to the main highway a few miles shorter. But in the long run, did it really matter? Why was he so desperate to get that land?

She'd called her dad's lawyer and left a message for him to call back.

She hadn't been up that way in a while, so she decided now was as good a time as any to trek the length of her property and take a look around at the end. See if she could discover what it was that put the gleam in

Malcolm Davis's eyes when he talked about that portion of land.

She prepared a backpack with water, protein bars and some snacks for Stella. There were no wolf packs within a good five-mile radius of the area, so she never worried that Stella would be singled out and attacked. But there were lynx and bears and all sorts of smaller animals that wouldn't mind threatening a wolf who was not accustomed to hunting bigger animals to survive. So Skylar also packed a Taser gun and a .30-06 rifle, for safety's sake.

"Come on, Stella," she called as she stepped out onto the deck and locked the patio door. "We're going for a hike."

Chapter Ten

Joe stood by as the emergency team pushed the stretcher into the back of the ambulance. One victim had been pulled out from the lake by a diver. He had been under water an estimated four minutes. He was unconscious, with a dangerously low heart rate, but they had hope and were in the process of resuscitating him even as the ambulance flashed its lights and took off out of the parking area before the boat landing.

Two patrol cars cordoned off the area, and three police officers were keeping onlookers from getting in the way. One officer talked to the boat driver with whom the Jet Ski had collided. He had abrasions on his arm and back—the Jet Ski had literally shaved across the side of his body as it had soared over his boat—but he was doing well otherwise.

Joe had helped the diving crew to secure the Jet Ski and get it on a tow truck. He also gave the sheriff's deputy, who had arrived after the victim had been pulled from the water, all the details. This accident would be their concern now.

When it was apparent his help was no longer needed,

he lingered, watching, while the crowd of gawkers thinned and the deputy ensured the beach was closed off. They would investigate, and if the Jet Ski driver survived, would question him to learn if it had simply been a machine malfunction, if he had been drunk or—well, there could be myriad reasons the collision had occurred.

Backing up and turning, Joe almost walked right into a Native American man who immediately patted him on the shoulder and nodded. Weathered skin creped his face and hands, and Joe guessed him to be about eighty, near Max's age.

"I hope you find the truth behind Max Owen's demise," the old man said to him. His eyes darted toward where they were cordoning off the beach with yellow caution tape, then back to Joe. "I know it's important to you to learn the truth, Joseph Cash."

Joe lifted a brow. He had no idea who this man was. Max had never mentioned any friends, but then, they hadn't chatted about things like that. He had belonged to a tribe, had grown up on a reservation, yet hadn't been in close contact with them since his midforties.

"You have no idea what Max Owen meant to me," Joe said.

"No, no I don't. But I do know what you meant to him, boy."

That statement cut into his heart. This man knew he'd had a relationship with Max?

The man bowed his head and toed the pebbled parking area with a boot. "We were in the same tribe. Didn't get to see Max as often as I liked. He preferred the wild, while I like the comforts of a sofa and public television. But we talked. And I know how proud he was that you embraced the wild in your soul."

Joe swallowed. He'd never been aware of Max's friends. But, of course, a man could not completely seclude himself from the world, even if he managed to do so more than half the year. "What can you tell me about Max's death?"

"Nothing. Just that you and I both know it wasn't an accident."

Joe nodded. He hadn't told anyone he was investigating the death. The obituary in the newspaper had listed it as accidental. So how could this old man know anything?

"My daughter works for the county morgue in Duluth," he provided quietly. "She filled me in when Max was brought in. Told me about the officer who insisted on an autopsy. Figured it could only be the young man Max had told me about. The one he calls the wolf whisperer."

Joe tugged in his lower lip with his teeth. Max was the only one who called him that. And yet, Skylar had spoken the same words a few days ago. It was a moniker that lifted his head and shoulders, and filled him with pride. And respect.

"Check with Davis Trucking," the old man said. "Max knew something. Something dangerous."

"What did he tell you?"

"Nothing. It was that one time we were walking along the road and one of those big blue trucks drove by. I just saw it on Max's face."

That was vague, but then Max had been a remarkably serene man. Rarely showed emotion. For someone to pick up on his unease by an expression, they had to know him better than a passing stranger.

"Was probably the eagles," he muttered.

"The what? Did you say eagles?" There it was again: *eagles*. The word seemed to flutter around this case like the elusive bird itself.

The man nodded.

"Tell me, please?"

With a resolute sigh, the man bowed his head, folding his hands before his gut, then said quietly, "It was Max who was always trying to get us to stop buying—well, you know."

"I don't know. That's why I'm asking. Buying what?"

"Eagle parts." The old man rubbed a hand at the back of his neck. "Feathers and talons. Our tribe is on the list to get the eagle parts the state confiscates."

Joe knew that any poached eagle remains were eventually turned over to the local tribes. They could apply for them. That prevented, or tended to prevent, poaching.

"But that list is long," the man said. "Sometimes takes years. And well, the contests pay big money."

"You just lost me. The contests?"

"The dance competitions at powwows. Fancy dance, grass, jingle. Traditional. Dancers can make a good living entering contests at the various powwows if they're willing to travel. If an eagle feather ever falls from a costume during a competition, the whole dance stops and a ceremony to pick it up is performed right then and there. The feather is treated as if it's a sacred, fallen warrior. It's a thing to see."

"And yet, you just insinuated those sacred feathers are obtained on the black market."

"Like I said, that waiting list is long. But Max finally talked some sense into the tribe elders. We don't do that anymore. Swear to it."

This was an angle of poaching Joe hadn't considered. He'd heard of it before, but hadn't put it into place during the investigation. Had Max known who was selling black market eagle parts and those people had, after losing the tribe as customers, shut Max up?

Joe needed to return to Max's campsite. To take it in again.

"Learn the truth," the old man said, and then with a nod, he wandered off toward a rusted pickup truck.

Joe's inner wild howled in defiance. He would learn the truth. Only then could he allow Max to rest peacefully.

"Davis Trucking," he repeated out loud.

It wasn't a surprise to hear that accusation. But how to crack the barrier Malcolm Davis had erected about his business and family, and learn the truth?

Perhaps a family member was his best entry. And Joe did know a family member quite well.

SWATTING AT A MOSQUITO, Skylar stood ten feet from the ragged red plastic flag that had been planted in the ground by her father years ago to demarcate the edge of his property. Half a dozen of the same were within her eyesight. One was bent and lying on the ground.

She was surprised any were still intact. The ones tied around trees tended to last longest, and she'd counted a few as she arrived here at the edge of her land.

Her land. It felt immense and also bittersweet to call it that. This had been her parents' land. No. Her father's land. Her mother didn't get to claim ownership since she had abandoned her family. It was as if she were dead to Skylar. She'd never wanted it to be that way, but the urge to seek out her mother had not been strong enough over the years.

Still, Skylar couldn't argue against a greater design and knew she was here in this world for a reason, and with a purpose. And that purpose was to be kind to animals and help those in need. Nothing else gave her such a feeling of completion. It wasn't even satisfaction or pride. She simply felt whole when helping a sick animal rise up to its healthy potential.

However, what with being shot at and her uncle's menace always looming close, it was difficult to concentrate on that which should garner her full attention.

Why was the end of the property such a golden goose to Malcolm? Sure, he could plow down the pine trees and clear the land to connect it to his property, which was only a quarter mile to the west. And if he laid down tarmac, paving a passage road, his trucks could pass through here instead of driving around the lake and out to County Road 7, a highway badly in need of reconstruction and paving due to incessant potholes. These old county highways were always the last on the list for repair.

To the east, the Enerson property nudged her land,

so Malcolm would also have to buy a sliver of land from them to make his road work. And if completed, it would be a secluded passage, hugged on both sides by tall conifers.

"Almost...secret," she muttered, as she envisioned the road. And if Davis Trucking did take this way through to Duluth or from Duluth, then they wouldn't have to pass through the truck weigh station up the highway. "Hmm..."

There was only one reason a truck wouldn't want to stop for inspection.

What had been in those freezers in the Davis warehouse that had upset the man so much he'd yelled at her as if she'd caught him stealing gold bullion from Fort Knox? He'd threatened her with a rifle. Why would an employee of a trucking company carry a rifle while on duty? Sure, they were entitled to security, but...it hadn't felt right at the time. Actually, Skylar had been terrified and couldn't have gotten out of there fast enough.

The Davis family, Malcolm's side, had been poaching for decades with little worry of repercussion. And while it should be enough for Skylar to want to talk to Joe and get him to stop such poaching from happening, a weird niggle in her stomach held her back. Malcolm was family. And her father had never reported his brother for that very reason. Family didn't do that to one another. Even if family had ruined her father's life, draining the family inheritance to start a trucking company and leaving no funds for his brother.

Her father had been a good man. Too good.

Was it time Skylar brushed off her father's benevolent influence and started fighting that which should have been stopped long ago?

Squatting and brushing her palm over a growth of blueberries, Skylar whistled. Stella, who had been wandering the woods nearby, hastened to her side.

"What do you think, Stella? Are we going to do it?"

If she did tell Joe everything she knew, then she could kiss Malcolm's offer to cosign and partially fund her shelter goodbye. She needed half-a-million dollars to get the shelter built and supplied. There was no way she could raise that herself, and she didn't have enough assets beyond the land to put down for a loan.

To fight her uncle and his empire would be like sacrificing her dream. But had the dream ever been possible in the first place?

She stood and started back toward the cabin, a good three-mile hike through the woods. Stella scampered ahead, always the leader.

She'd visit the lawyer today. There had to be some way to do this on her own.

Chapter Eleven

"You're not going to like hearing this. Your mother is still a legal owner of the property," the lawyer announced after he'd set the Merlin Davis file on the dark walnut table before him.

Hans Svendson offered Skylar ice water, which she sipped while wincing. She sat at the edge of the overstuffed chair pulled up to the conference table, feeling the weight of the wealth that had furnished this small yet luxurious office. It was in the man's home. He didn't set up shop in town. He lived on a fifty-acre estate with security fences and cameras.

"How is that possible?" she asked, sliding the water glass aside to lean forward. "She—we don't even know where she is. She could be dead, for all I know."

"The will did give you ownership of the property," the lawyer said, "but that was dependent on both your parents' deaths. I'm sorry I didn't dig this out immediately after your father's death, Skylar."

"I just assumed, since he had given me that note saying I owned the land…"

"Yes, I remember that. Unfortunately, it's not legally

binding. The original will holds precedence. As long as one of your parents is still alive—your mother—she holds half the property rights."

"That's crazy." Skylar sat back in the chair. "Again. How do we even know she is alive? Isn't there some sort of statute on how long that will can remain in effect if one of the parties is AWOL?"

"Until she is proven dead—and I did a quick search for Dorothy Davis online, no death certificate—then she is still considered a property holder. I'm sorry, Skylar. Merlin was such a good man. I wish he had made changes to the will before his death, but it dates back almost twenty years."

When she was ten and her mother hadn't yet abandoned them.

"What am I supposed to do about this? I was hoping to build a shelter, but if the land isn't even completely mine, I can't sell part of it." She closed her eyes. How could this be possible?

Then she opened them in a flash. "She can't be aware of ownership. She would have claimed it by now."

The lawyer shrugged. "That's possible. And remember, you do own half."

"Which half?"

Hans shrugged. "It's not so simple as drawing a line down the middle. Or it could be. It may be as simple as tracking Dorothy down and asking for her to hand complete ownership to you. Then I can help you see to using the land as collateral for a loan. Or maybe you should consider asking Malcolm—"

"Never," she cut him off. "You know my dad and his

brother were at odds. If Malcolm ever found out I don't own all the land… You can't tell him."

"He's not a client of mine. And I have no reason to tell him anything. I don't much like the man myself. I remember the struggles your father went through when Malcolm was trying to buy half his land from him."

"My dad was dead set against forming any business that might harm the environment. Farming, with all its chemicals, was out. And trucking, with all the diesel fuel, was a big no-no. He was an artist."

The lawyer nodded. "I actually bought one of his photographs. Still have it up in the living room. That man had an eye for beauty. Well. So now you know. Would you like me to put you in contact with someone who can locate your mother for you? I know a private investigator."

"Not right now. This is all new and shocking to me. I have to take a while to…" Skylar blew out a breath. "You know."

"Yes, I understand. But you will call me if you need anything, yes?"

She nodded and stood. He led her out to the front door and she headed to the truck.

The day could not get any worse.

JOE KNOCKED ON Skylar's front door and waited. The setting sunlight shimmered through the trees surrounding her house. This was a gorgeous, peaceful plot of land. Something he wouldn't mind owning himself. And he would have such a property someday. It would be a long yet fulfilling journey to make his dream come true.

He wanted to share that dream with someone. It was difficult to stand here now, on the doorstep of a woman with whom he could consider spending that future, because—well, because of what Cole Pruitt had told him.

The door opened and Joe noticed Skylar swiftly wipe a teardrop from her cheek. Her eyes were red.

"What is it?" He stepped across the threshold and slid his hands along her arms. She wobbled, and he steadied her.

"Stella," she said. "She's not doing well."

"Where is she? Are you okay, Skylar? What's happened?" He bent to study her face, and she nodded and managed a half wince, half smile.

"I'm fine. Heartbroken. Stella is out on the deck. I found her a few hours ago at the edge of the yard. She'd been vomiting and has a fever."

He slid a hand into hers and walked through the house toward the patio doors. Outside on the deck, lying on the big dog bed that was Stella's perch, he found the wolf. She didn't lift her head as Joe approached, and he could see her chest rising heavily.

He dropped Skylar's hand and knelt on the deck, cautious not to scare the wolf and sensing she was in her own world right now. Fighting something terrible within.

"How did this happen?"

Skylar settled next to him and stroked a hand over Stella's coat. "I found her struggling to stand and was able to get her up here. She's been whimpering, and her heartbeats are irregular. But I think the extreme effects are beginning to subside. I was able to give her an IV of fluids and activated charcoal to induce vomiting. I think she was poisoned."

"Poisoned?" Joe's heart thudded at the word. Why was every living being around him lately falling victim to poison? Of course, the forest was not the safest place; it was filled with poisonous plants. He met Skylar's gaze. "You got oleander or milkweed in the area?"

"She knows to stay away from the milkweed. I don't believe it was a plant. There were undigested chunks of animal meat on the ground near her. I think…"

Joe bit his lip and shook his head because he knew what had happened. "Someone did this purposely," he ground out tightly. "The bastards. Who would do this? What is going on, Skylar? First someone shoots at you and now they've sunk to the bottom rung by harming an animal? And Max…"

"Max?"

He shook his head. It couldn't be related. He was still out of sorts after talking with the man near the drowning incident about Max. He had to keep the investigations separate until there was good reason to pair them. "It's an investigation on the side. Not related to this. Maybe."

"Can we discuss the bad stuff later?" She bent and gave Stella a hug. "I just want to be here for her. She isn't seizing anymore, so I want to watch her for now."

Skylar curled up before the wolf and put her face right next to Stella's. The wolf's eyes were closed, but she nudged her nose against Skylar's cheek.

Joe blew out a breath. The anger in him wanted to

rage and kick something. His better senses told him both Skylar and Stella needed him to be calm and reassuring. This was another puzzle in the case he'd stumbled onto, and he suspected it was all connected to the local poaching. Right now, however, all that mattered was seeing to Stella.

And securing evidence.

"Where did you find her?" he asked quietly. "I want to gather evidence. Have it analyzed by the lab. It could help in your treatment, as well."

"Yes, I can plan further treatment for her. Right down there, at the edge of the clearing by the lake. Thank you, Joe. I had no idea you were stopping by. Was there a reason?"

"Doesn't matter now." He kissed her on the crown of the head, and the moment felt bittersweet. He preferred such intimate contact under better circumstances. "I'm going to grab some evidence bags from my truck and take a look around in the woods. Call if you need me, okay?"

"I will." She clasped his hand and squeezed. "I'm glad you're here. I…needed someone to be with me."

Joe understood how difficult it was for her to say such a thing. Strong, independent and fierce, Skylar Davis had never needed anyone. It was sad that her armor was cracking because of outside forces.

He was glad he'd arrived when he did.

Chapter Twelve

Lying beside Stella on the deck, Skylar let her hand rest on the wolf's stomach. Her breathing was still shallower than normal, but she felt she was going to survive this. Strychnine, which had once been commonly used by poachers, usually worked quickly, within a few hours. Other poisons could take up to forty-eight hours and cause a slow, cruel death. Stella would need to be watched through the night.

From her vantage point, she'd watched Joe gather evidence from the shore where she'd found Stella. Then he'd wandered into the forest and disappeared into the thickness of maple, oak, birch and brush. Now and then the beam from his flashlight lit up the darkening woods. What luck that he had arrived when he had. She'd been frantic and worried over Stella, but had known she needed to gather evidence so she could later determine exactly what had happened to the wolf.

Her gut told her the poisoning had been a purposeful act. And she'd sensed Joe's entire body tense when she'd told him her suspicion. The man cared about wildlife and carried as strong a conviction about keeping animals safe as she did. She loved that about him. And she knew he probably felt the hurt as much as she did. That genuine kindness placed him a notch above all other men in her book. He was strong, smart and, by nature, a protector. And she had pushed that away in favor of what?

She'd thought she was in love with Cole. The man had been a high school track star, loved singing eighties hair band tunes at the top of his lungs, always had a cooler of Budweiser ready for a fishing adventure on the lake, and had told her she was beautiful and brought her flowers and made her eggs at midnight. He'd been hyper, and was never one to sit still. Opposite of her. He was different and new and everything she'd never thought she'd want in a man.

Cole had been a means to distance herself, really. He had not threatened her independence and had seemed like a good fit at the time.

How she could have ever thought she could be happy with someone like that was beyond her now. She'd been a fool. And it had been too close on the heels of her father's death. Grief had altered her perception of her real needs and wants. And because of her misdirected need for companionship—any sort of connection to a man—she had gotten caught in something bigger than her. And terrible.

She had to tell Joe what she knew. But would he trust her if she did so?

Becky popped up onto the deck and wandered over to peck at Stella's fur. The chicken sensed the wolf was not well, and she didn't pester her overmuch. Instead, she hopped up onto the low wood table and nestled down to roost next to Skylar's cowboy hat in her bright red sweater. She closed her eyes, keeping vigil.

Footsteps ascended the deck stairway and Skylar sat up. She patted the deck beside her and Joe sat down. Stella was sleeping erratically.

"I found a few chunks of meat down by the lake. Not sure what kind though. Could be fowl," he said. "Looks like someone might have pulled up to your dock in a boat and tossed it to shore. There were no footprints. I've bagged the evidence and will take it in to the forensic lab."

"Please make sure they forward that report to me. I'll be able to better treat Stella if I know what she's ingested."

"I will. How you holding up?"

"I'm better now that you're here."

He clasped her hand, and she reacted by tilting her head onto his shoulder. He smelled like pine and wet scrub that he must have stomped with his boots. Delicious. And he was...still. So unlike Cole. It was a difference she'd recognized easily when choosing Cole. But only now did she understand the implications of going against what her heart really needed.

And it hurt.

"She going to be okay?" His voice softened and cracked.

"I hope so. The best treatment is to watch her. She's a fighter. She survived the trap when most pups would have quickly perished or been eaten by a predator."

"Stella gets around well on three legs. She is a marvel. I'm here for you, sweetie," he said to the wolf. "You want me to get you something to drink?"

"That would be nice. I was thinking about camping out here by her tonight."

"I'll be right back. Tea good?"

"There's brandy in the cupboard above the fridge."

She caught his smile on his profile. "Brandy it is."

Ten minutes later Joe reappeared, boots off and padding in his socks, jeans hems scuffing the deck boards. He set a glass of brandy down before her, then began to lay out the blanket he had grabbed from the back of the couch. It was a quilt her grandmother had made for her when she was a teenager, fashioned from squares of fabric saved over the years from dresses her mother—Skylar's great-grandmother—had made for her. She loved this blanket and used it all the time.

"Okay if I put this here?" he asked. "It's a nice blanket. Maybe you don't want it out here?"

"No, that's good, thank you. And you even grabbed a pillow. Why are you so sweet?"

He shrugged. "Just doing what you need someone to do for you right now. You shouldn't have to struggle with this stuff yourself. You focus on Stella. But…is it okay if I hang around and hold watch with you?"

"Do you want to?"

"There's nothing I would rather be doing. The evidence won't be looked at until morning anyway, so I have no need to leave or report in. And I do need to punch the clock once in a while. Can't work twenty-four/seven. That is, if Becky doesn't mind."

The chicken cooed contentedly without opening her

eyes. A sure sign of approval. Skylar patted the deck beside her.

He sat on the blanket before Stella, and Skylar moved in next to him, offering him a sip from her glass. He'd filled it half-full with the aromatic amber brandy. More than she'd ever drink. When he took a hearty swallow, she felt more grateful than shocked. A brandy buzz might be just the thing to soften her anxiety right now. *And* her nerves about sitting so close to Joe.

Below in the grass, crickets chirped, and the haunting call of a loon punctuated the still night. The tree canopy opened in the center of her yard to reveal stars speckling the sky.

Skylar pointed upward. "That's the best part about living away from a city."

"No doubt about it. I believe there are some city folk who have never seen a star in the night sky. Too bad for them."

She tilted her head against his shoulder and he took her hand and kissed the back of it. The moment felt intimate, private. Something more than two concerned adults holding vigil over a sick wolf.

Skylar looked up and Joe was already staring down at her. She smiled at his shadowed grin.

"What?" he asked, like the kid who had been caught sneaking something he wasn't supposed to.

"Have we ever made out? I mean, more than kissing?"

"I would remember doing something like that with you, Skylar. You know our timing was always off."

"Yes, and I regret that now."

"You do?"

She nodded. "But not even on that night…?" That dreaded night he'd refused her suggestion they have sex. And she'd been punishing herself, more than him, for it ever since.

"Not even." He winced. "When I make out with you, Skylar, I want to be fully present and not drunk."

"You get drunk all that often, Joseph Cash?" She knew the answer, but it was a gentle tease; she couldn't resist.

"Nope. I like to get drunk on nature."

Could the man be any more sexy than he was right now? Well, for sure his calendar spread, with the bared abs and wide shoulders, and oh, that come-get-me smile, had been the hottest month of the year. And she hadn't made out with him when she'd had the chance? Mercy.

She tilted up her head. Their gazes met. Skylar was pretty sure a couple stars twinkled in Joe's eyes. Without another thought, she said, "Kiss me."

Showing no reluctance, he bowed to her and his mouth met hers. The sigh she'd been holding in escaped in a sweet rush of desire. His lips played softly against hers, finding a moment to stay, to build up the heat, and then brushing here or there for a heartbeat of connection.

Sliding her hand up the front of his shirt, she glided it over the hard muscles beneath and landed on the warmth of his skin just under his jaw. Stubble tickled her fingertips. Pushing her fingers around his neck and up through his short hair, she clutched and held him to her for a longer kiss. A dive into a starry night that she never wanted to end.

The faintest taste of brandy only teased her deeper. And when his arm wrapped across her back, she thought surely he was holding her to this earth, this moment, with a sure and confident promise of safety. The spread of his fingers against her side nudged just under her breast and she wanted to ease into him, to feel him touching her, but she cautioned herself that her eager need was probably a reaction to her grief over Stella.

Her and grief. She didn't handle that well when it came to getting her desires met. Keep it in the now and take it slow, she thought. She didn't want to scare him away a second time.

When they parted, he bowed his forehead to hers and they breathed in each other's warmth. Her heartbeats thudded faster than Stella's, and Skylar cast a look to the wolf. Her chest rose and fell at a more normal pace. She was sleeping peacefully now.

"That," Joe said softly, "is a kiss I will never forget."

And at that moment Stella shifted and placed her paw on Joe's thigh.

"I think she approves," Skylar offered.

"That means more to me than you can imagine."

"Animals are a good judge of people."

"That they are. She trusts you to take care of her. The two of you together are good. You are her person."

"And she's my girl. You have any pets, Joe?"

"Nope. That's not my thing. Never home long enough to care for one properly. Max always taught me…" He looked aside and closed his eyes. "It's nothing."

"Who is Max? You mentioned him before."

"He's the Native American man they found lying roadside a few weeks ago. I'm sure you heard about it."

"Oh, right. News reports said he'd eaten some poisonous berries or something and tried to walk for help but it was too late?"

"Max was smarter than that. He was poisoned," Joe said tightly. "But not by his own doing."

"You think so?"

"I know so. And now…" He spread his fingers through Stella's coat. "You said you didn't want to talk about this. Right now we need to focus on Stella. But you need to know, with her poisoning I'm more suspicious than ever. Something's going on, Skylar. And I will get to the bottom of it."

Joe woke to bright sunlight. And an aching back. What was up with his strange sleeping situations of late that found him either in a car or on a deck?

Skylar had reentered his life, that was what was up. And he didn't regret one moment of it.

Shifting on the deck to his side, he saw Stella lying on her cushion. Head bowed and resting on her paws, her gold eyes held him steadily. And…her tail wagged.

"You feeling better, Stella?"

The wolf whined softly, which didn't sound so much painful as an agreement to her better state. He ruffled his palm over her coat behind her ears and the wolf rolled to her back, exposing her belly to him. Such an amazing sign of trust. Joe leaned on an elbow and gave her the belly rub she sought.

"You've stolen my heart, you know that, sweetie? What is it about you Davis females?" He lowered his voice to a whisper. "You do know I like your person, right? I've liked her for a long time. But... I'm worried about her. I know you've been taking care of her, just as well as she took care of you last night. But I sense something isn't right with her."

The wolf stretched out her paw and rested it over his wrist, as if to say *You're right*.

"You want to help me help your person?"

He bowed his head and Stella licked his hair. She had made it through the night, but she would still need some tender loving care until all the poison was purged from her system. No doubt Skylar was on it. Wherever she was.

He looked around the deck and down across the yard. Off toward the chicken coop, he spied Skylar's cowboy hat. Then he checked his watch—6:30 a.m.

"Too early." He lay back and eyed the wolf. "Let's catch a few more winks, what do you say?"

Stella laid her muzzle on his arm, and the twosome drifted off in shared slumber.

SKYLAR TOOK JOE'S coffee mug from him as he skipped down the front steps. Stella sat beside her, watching. She was still weak and would need a great deal of rest, but her tail wagged and she whined at Joe's leaving.

"Someone is going to miss you," Skylar said.

"I'll miss her, too, but I have to go. That evidence bag." He thumbed toward his truck. "That's not going to last much longer if the day gets any hotter."

"Thank you. Again." Skylar tilted up on her tiptoes and kissed him.

Joe pulled away from it and put his hands on her shoulders. He didn't want to kiss her again? What was up with that? Had last night been a fluke? Both of them had been tired and he'd reacted in a moment of silent weariness? What was it with the man and his refusal to encourage intimacy between the two of them?

"I, uh…" He bowed his head and then lifted it to look directly in her eyes. "You and me? This is something I've thought about for a long time. But you know, back then, when we were on different schedules? I've always known you were out of my league."

"Out of my—"

"It's just how I feel, Skylar. And I realized over this past year that you made your choice. And it wasn't me. So, I gotta go." He had turned to head to the truck when he paused suddenly. "What the hell?"

The goat was performing a dance on the hood of Joe's vehicle.

Skylar waved it off as usual goat antics. "She's playing. Just ask her politely and she'll get down."

Joe quirked a brow, as if considering how one goes about politely asking something of a goat. "Seriously?"

Skylar nodded and gestured for him to approach the goat. He did, slowly.

"What's her name?"

"Beyoncé!"

"Right. Of course. An obvious name for a goat. Beyoncé."

The goat stomped the hood playfully as Joe stood

there, hands spread as if to catch her. Skylar winced, hoping she wouldn't dent it. The man finally gripped the goat carefully and set her on the ground. She bounced off, bleating happily.

Joe waved as he backed the truck away.

Skylar clutched her clasped hands over her freshly wounded heart. He thought she was too good for him? How ridiculous. And she hadn't made a choice between—

Though she could completely understand how he would feel that way. Fine. She had made a sort of choice. She knew it, just as he did.

She swore softly. How to tell the man she had been wrong? To make him understand that she simply needed him?

Chapter Thirteen

"Interesting." Lucy, the forensics analyst, set the slide before Joe and crossed her arms dramatically, pausing while he waited for her to continue.

"Yeah?" he finally prompted.

"That is eagle meat. Laced with strychnine."

"The same poison…" Joe's voice trailed off.

"That killed Max Owen." She nodded when he lifted his head abruptly. "I know about that case. Heard about the conservation officer who paid for the old man to have an autopsy because he didn't believe it was an accident. It was still ruled accidental."

"It wasn't," Joe said. "I knew Max. He wasn't that stupid."

"Some of those old Native Americans really know their flora and fauna, but everyone makes mistakes, Cash."

"Strychnine is not a natural substance, is it?"

"It's from the nux vomica tree, The seeds make the poison. It's not a plant native to Minnesota, but a person can get that stuff by bulk if they know the right people."

"And if they're looking to poison wildlife." Joe tightened his jaw. "And now, two weeks following Max's death, another strychnine poisoning? Don't you find that suspicious?"

Lucy shrugged. "In the overall scheme of things? No. Like you said, hunters still use that nasty stuff to poison wildlife. Farmers use it to kill wolves. But if you narrow it down to the small area you've been investigating lately, then yes, I agree there's something fishy going on. The poison was definitely injected into those meat samples you brought in."

The satisfaction Joe felt at having Lucy corroborate his suspicion was short-lived. "Had Max Owen taken in the poison from surface contact or internally?"

"I don't know."

"Can you look it up?"

"Should be able to." Lucy tapped at her laptop on the short desk in the forensic lab van. She finally nodded and said, "It was contact. So he touched meat, or something with the poison on it. Think he was into poaching?"

"Definitely not."

"And now another incident of strychnine poisoning."

"Eagle meat," Joe repeated. "You know what kind of eagle?"

Lucy shook her head. "Hard to determine. But I do know eagle meat on sight. I've seen it more times in the lab than a person should have to. Poor birds. So someone was trying to poison the—did you say it was a wolf?"

"Yes, Stella. She's a rescue animal living with an animal rehab therapist right now."

"You think a poacher went after the wolf?"

Joe shook his head. "Not sure. I think someone was sending a threatening message to the woman who cares for the wolf. Now I just have to figure out if that someone also sent the same message to Max Owen."

Lucy leaned against the stainless steel lab table. "I get the occasional animal in here. I've seen this same poison in the bloodstream before. Maybe…recently?" She turned, jiggled the computer mouse and started clicking away.

"In this area?" Joe asked. "I've been investigating about a fifty-mile range with Checker Hill as the center point."

"Any leads yet?"

"I have my suspicions. Davis Trucking employs truckers from about the same radius."

"You mess with that company, they'll bring you down, Cash."

"Why do you say that? What do you know about them?"

"Same thing everyone knows. They own some of the law enforcement in this county. Can get away with virtually anything. Likely even murder."

And had they gotten away with Max Owen's murder? "They don't own me," Joe said.

"Here." Lucy turned the laptop so Joe could read the screen over her shoulder. "Last month, one of your fellow conservation officers, Robbie Anderson, brought in a burlap bag of bald eagles. Five of them. Taken down with strychnine-laced squirrel meat. We knew they'd been poached."

"Did Robbie find the source?"

Lucy shook her head. "I haven't heard from him. And he hasn't been in since then."

"Thanks, Lucy. I'll give him a call." Joe headed for the door but stopped when Lucy called to him.

"Be careful, Cash. I like it when you visit. I'd hate to see those visits stop. I'll see you soon," she said, and then gave him a wink.

It always startled Joe when women flirted with him.

He wandered out, sorting through the facts he'd just learned.

Max had touched something covered with strychnine. Could it have been an eagle? That made little sense; Max wouldn't have had reason to do such a thing.

This case was growing bigger. He pulled out his cell phone, called Dispatch and asked them to patch him in to Robbie's phone. The call went to voice mail. He was probably out in the field. He left a message, asking him to call him about the poisoned bald eagles. "I've got a couple poisoning cases that are similar. We need to share notes."

THE CAMP WHERE Max had spent his summers had been cleared away by the crime-scene unit. It had been little more than a tent, a cookstove and a carved oak stump that the old man liked to sit on as he was whittling.

Joe inhaled a breath and wandered the area, determined to see what all the others had missed. There were so many footprints belonging to others who had no idea of the kindness of the old man. They'd remember him only as the victim or the dead man. The Native American living off the grid who had likely eaten something poisonous. Fool.

Squatting near where the fire ring remained, a circle of fist-sized rocks coated in soot, Joe took a branch and stirred the ashes. He wasn't looking for anything in particular. Or was he? Surely Forensics had poked and prodded with the same goal. All that remained was heavy white ash and chunks of charcoal.

Joe pressed his fingers over the eagle talon at his neck. It felt cool. His only token from a man who had taught him so much. He'd never told his parents about Max. Now it didn't feel necessary, though they should know their son had found a mentor in that great man.

Maybe he'd bring it up at the next family dinner. Mom called in the crew for those at least one Sunday a month. Of course, it might worry his mother that he was only mentioning his relationship with Max now. He didn't want to upset her. There was nothing to be upset about, but people went places in their imaginations when they heard things like a ten-year-old boy spending days in the wild with a stranger.

How might Max have gotten something laced with strychnine in hand? Someone had to have planted something in the campsite. Or had he found it while out wandering? If it had been an eagle, or animal meat of some sort, had it consumed the poison by feeding on a trapped animal? It was possible. Yet surely Max would have approached a dead bird or even bait cautiously, suspicious over its death until he could be sure it was a natural death and safe to handle.

Maybe.

Joe knew Max would sometimes eat a small animal he'd found if it was newly dead, and not sick or infested with insects. He didn't survive the summers on dandelion tea and blueberries.

After standing up, Joe wandered the grassy circumference that demarcated Max's little circle in the midst of the forest. A taconite slab with a sheered wall grew up ten feet on the west side. The rock was rusty red and black. He loved that stone, and Max had showed him how to chip off slices and hammer the edge to form a rudimentary blade. Fun stuff for a teenager. He still had one of those caveman blades, as he'd called it, somewhere in his office.

It was easy to see, from the footsteps of the crime team, when they had decided they'd searched far enough, so Joe crossed the crushed grass and wandered into the forest. He stopped before each tree trunk and pressed his boot down on the loamy earth. Max had a tendency to bury bones and organic matter such as compost. At the third birch tree, his foot crushed tender earth that had been previously disturbed.

Joe squatted and prodded the earth with his fingers. There was something buried there. He pulled out his knife and used it to dig, being careful not to point it, instead using the edge so he wouldn't damage any evidence. About six inches down, he uncovered something that made him swear.

"An eagle."

Chapter Fourteen

Skylar opened the front door and invited Joe in. She stepped back, lifting an arm to brace across her chest. He sensed a touch of coolness to her demeanor. He'd pulled away from her kiss this morning because he'd remembered what Cole Pruitt had said to him about Skylar knowing more than she was letting on.

Joe handed Skylar the forensic lab report. "The poison was strychnine. The meat was soaked in it. But you'll never guess what kind of meat it was."

Skylar glanced at the report then gave him a shocked look. "Bald eagle?"

"Bastards are poaching bald eagles. I knew they were taking wolves, deer and smaller animals without a license, but the eagle brings this to a new low."

"Is taking down a bald eagle still a federal offense?" Skylar asked. "Because I'd really like to see those guys go down. Especially since they went after Stella."

"Those guys?" Joe hooked his hands at his hips and faced her directly. "Would that be your family, Skylar?"

"My family? My dad is dead, Joe, and you know that. My mother up and left long ago. I'm on my own."

He did recall that Skylar's mom had left her when she'd been a young teenager. She certainly had her reasons to keep people at a distance.

"You know who I'm talking about. Malcolm Davis and the Davis Trucking empire. You don't consider them family?"

She gave a dismissive nod. "I suppose they are, but I don't talk to Malcolm unless I have to. And I generally don't have to."

Frustrated at her seeming ability to skirt around anything regarding the one person high on his suspects list, Joe pleaded, "Skylar, what aren't you telling me? How long have you been involved with what Malcolm is up to?"

"In-involved? Oh, no, Joe, you've got that wrong. I don't work for—you think *I'm* involved with the poaching?"

Her body language screamed *offense* as she shifted from foot to foot, stepping back, then forward, not sure what to do with her hands, which eventually formed fists.

"How dare you?" she finally blurted out. "I would never."

"But you know they are poachers."

"Everyone knows that. For heaven's sake—Joe, I *rescue* animals for a living. Do you think I'd be so heartless as to purposely take an animal's life?"

No, he did not. And yet. "I talked to Cole Pruitt yesterday. Found him out on Lake Seraphim. He told me that after learning what you were involved in, he was the one to leave you at the altar."

Her jaw dropped open.

"And he said you hooked him up with Malcolm's crew. That's the reason he left you, because apparently you were not the woman he thought you were."

She stared at him with an openmouthed glare. Growling, Skylar stomped out of the living room and into the kitchen. There she paced twice, hands to her hips, then headed to the back of the house. She stopped at the patio doors, turned and lifted a finger as if to punctuate a statement, then shook her head and spun away from him.

"Skylar, talk to me."

Her growl was laced with frustration, and she tossed up her hands in defeat. "Do you really believe all of that, Joe?"

To see her reaction, he didn't now. And he hadn't when Cole had said it to him out on the lake. Well, he'd had a moment of doubt, which was why he'd had to ask the questions. But, of course, Skylar could not be a part of the poaching going on in the area. He had only to look at Stella to know what a kind heart Skylar had.

And yet. "Malcolm has a lot of control over things in this county. Some say he might even have a hand in local law enforcement."

"He does, and I wouldn't put it past him to have a few dirty cops in his pocket." She slammed her hands to her hips, her head bowed. She wasn't about to look at him. Joe could feel anger radiate off her. Or was it fear?

"Does he control you, Skylar?"

"Never. He's tried, but—oh, hell."

Joe rushed over and took Skylar by the shoulders,

turning her to face him. "He's tried? What? What has he done or said to you, Skylar? Please, you can tell me. I want to help."

"It's just…it's not what you think with the poaching, Joe."

"Then what should I think?"

Her expression showed she struggled with fear and anger and a pining sort of trust right now. She wanted to confide in him; he could sense it. He took her hands and held them and didn't say anything more. He wanted her to know he was there for her.

Finally Skylar said, "Malcolm has been after a parcel of land since my dad was alive. Dad refused to sell. Wanted to keep it pristine. You know what a tree hugger he was. But lately Malcolm has been putting pressure on me to sell. Even offered to cosign on a loan I can't seem to get for the shelter I want to build. At least, that was the plan. Until Cole and I, well…he was going to co-sign. But after I learned that he was involved with Malcolm I broke it off."

"Cole and Malcolm?" Joe nodded. That was not a big leap to take. Not after what he'd witnessed on the lake. Cole had been drinking hard liquor; that wasn't his MO. Something had changed with his former friend, and drastically.

"And then I learned that my mother actually owns half the land, and now I don't know what to think of anything."

"Your mother? I thought she was gone?"

"She is. Haven't heard a peep from her since I was twelve. Joe, I talked to my dad's former lawyer, thinking he might advise me on how to go about getting this shelter business begun without having to resort to taking Malcolm's assistance. Upon reviewing my father's will, we learned that my mother actually owns half the land. Dad hadn't rewritten the will after she left us."

"Oh man, that's tough."

"Right. But it has nothing to do with what you're investigating. I shouldn't have brought it up, I—"

Joe pulled her into a hug. "You can talk to me about anything, Skylar. I mean it."

"I know you do, and…" She pulled out of the hug and managed a brief smile. "I love you for that. Honestly. Ah! This whole thing is driving me crazy," Skylar said. "I just want peace. And I want to be able to walk out into my backyard without fear of being shot at because I may have seen something."

"You saw something? Where? At Malcolm's place? What did you see, Skylar?"

"I don't know. I was looking for Malcolm, going to give him a piece of my mind regarding finding yet another trapped animal on my property, and I walked into a warehouse full of crates. And…freezers. I was threatened with a rifle to leave and never tell a soul."

"Who threatened you?"

"I don't know. I rarely go on Davis Trucking property. One of the employees. He was tall. Had red hair. I ran. Fast. I'm sure that's why someone shot at me. They were sending me a warning to keep quiet. Of course, I don't know what I would talk to anyone about. Like I said, I don't know what was in those freezers."

"There's only one thing I can imagine that would be

kept in a freezer. Animal parts. That bastard leaves carcasses all over the county, and hires his own truckers to set and monitor traps. I've learned that much. But I'm missing something. Something big. Something that has recently put you in harm's way. And...Max."

Skylar tilted her head. "You think the old man saw something, too? That he was silenced?"

"It's beginning to feel like it. I went back to Max's camp. Found a buried eagle carcass. I just dropped it off at the forensic lab, and I'm guessing it's laced with strychnine. It had to be what killed Max."

"He put poison on an eagle?"

"No. I think... Forensics said he had to have handled it quite a bit to absorb the poison through his skin and into his system. And Max had a reverence for all animals. I'm guessing he found the dead eagle, probably held it close, whispered to his people for it. Might have stroked its wings. Then he buried it. The whole time he would have never been aware of the poison."

"That's awful. But if he found it dead somewhere..."

"I think it was placed for him to find it. Probably by the one who would be most affected now that Max had convinced his tribe to stop buying black market eagle parts."

"Malcolm?"

Joe nodded and raked his fingers through his hair. "Still need a viable link. But I'll find it. I'm close. I can feel it."

"Malcolm told me Cole had taken down an eagle to show his alliance to him. That was the reason I called off the wedding."

"Why would Malcolm tell you that? You'd think he'd want to keep the illegal doings of all his employees as quiet as possible. Maybe he wanted to break the two of you up?"

Skylar shrugged. "I don't waste any time trying to put myself in the mind of that man. He was never kind to my dad."

"And yet, you avoided telling me all this until now. You could have said something that night I came over when I got the call."

Skylar exhaled heavily. "It's a family thing, Joe. I need to get beyond the whole 'don't rat on the family' mind-set. I have gotten beyond it. I'm tired of it all. And then to learn about my mother owning half the land? Like I said, I'm ready to end it all. So whatever you need to know about Malcolm, I'll tell you. But I've said all that I do know."

"I appreciate you finally trusting me enough to tell me. Is there anything I can do to make things better about the situation with your mom?"

She shook her head. "I've got to decide if I want a private investigator to track her down to see what she wants to do about the land. But if I just let it go, maybe she'll never return and I'll have the land. I mean, maybe she doesn't know she owns half. I have to think about it."

"Tough thoughts."

"Worthy of another few sips of brandy, for sure."

"You know Cole has been hitting the hard stuff?" Joe asked.

"I didn't. What do you mean?"

"I smelled whiskey on his breath when I talked to him on the lake."

"But he's a beer guy. I wonder if he's stressed-out? A guy can't work for Malcolm and retain his sanity. Or so I'd imagine."

"Yeah. I worry about him."

"Even after he stole the girl?"

Joe smirked. "Even after. You were never mine to steal."

"I wish I had been."

He tilted his head in wonder at that statement. And just when he thought now would be an appropriate time to kiss her, he remembered that something was missing. "Where is Stella? I expected a big ol' wolfie greeting."

"She's…" Skylar stepped away from him and poked her head out onto the deck to scan the yard. She called for the wolf a few times. "That's odd. She always comes when I call."

"Think she's out hunting?"

"She's too domesticated. She prefers her meat and kibble in a bowl. This is weird." She walked toward the forest edge. "I have to go look for her."

"I'm right behind you. Does she do this often? Wander off?"

"She usually stays close to home, and only goes out when I do. And she's still not feeling one hundred percent. So maybe… Stella!" Skylar stepped into the brushy woods.

Joe followed. If Skylar suspected something wasn't right, then he trusted her instincts. And if the Davis family was involved, he wouldn't stop until they paid dearly for their crimes.

"Let me," Joe said as he pushed ahead of Skylar. "I've been tracking wolves for a decade."

"Sure, but I know Stella." She moved aside for him on a narrow path that was tapering quickly and ended abruptly in a copse of birch.

Joe knelt and studied the ground. Here were patches of loam and mud and… He spied a very distinctive wolf track owing to the animal having only three paws to move on. The tracks led to the left, through a less grassy area and between two trees. He followed carefully, hunched over to keep his head low and nose closer to the ground. When tracking a wolf, it was wisest to breathe what they had breathed and see what they had seen. And from this vantage point, he spied the glimmer from the lake to the left.

The tracks paralleled the lake, so he followed.

Behind him Skylar suddenly let out a wolfie howl. Joe stopped and turned to her. She put a finger to her lips. Not three seconds later a wolf returned the howl. It sounded distant. Wolves could communicate miles away from one another. And it wasn't a surprise they had answered Skylar's call.

"It's not her," she said, and walked ahead of him, her head down, scanning the grass and branches and tree roots that would trip a person not paying attention.

He put out an arm to slow her and slipped in front of her. "Let me do this, please."

"She's *my* wolf," Skylar snapped.

"I know what I'm doing. I have a way with wolves."

"I know you do. But she'll scent me, so I need to be in front."

Ready to argue the ridiculousness of that statement, Joe forced himself to hold his tongue. Skylar was upset. Stella was missing, and she was still recovering from being poisoned. If they wanted to find her, they needed to work together.

"You know of any rendezvous points in the area? Does she often venture beyond your land?"

Skylar resumed walking, pushing aside branches and avoiding the pine boughs with ease. "There is an old rendezvous near the lake about half a mile ahead. You think she went there? She avoids that area because it's former pack territory. I think she can still scent them and maybe misses them."

"She might be trying to return home. Wolves are social animals."

"I know that. I don't need a basic wolf class from you."

She stomped ahead, and Joe fisted his hands. She was being obstinate. He wanted to give her some freedom, but who exactly was he dealing with here? Whatever she had seen in the Davis warehouse had to have been illegal if she'd been threatened. Twice. Could those freezers have contained eagle parts?

Crouching again, he eyed the ground and low grass, no longer picking out the tracks. Joe stopped and swung a look to the side, and then the other side. Stella had not gone this direction. She'd veered off…somewhere.

"Stop, Skylar," he whispered. "She's not that way. I've lost her tracks."

Skylar swung around, and the emotions playing on her face startled Joe. Was she near tears?

"I don't know what I'll do if I lose her, Joe."

"You won't," he said quickly, but wasn't as sure of the reply as he wanted to be. "Come here."

"I need to find her!"

"Just give me one minute. Come here, Skylar."

She wandered over and he pulled her into a hug, which she resisted at first, but then her body sank against his and she sniffled tears. He didn't know what to say, so he simply held her and allowed her to cry, to pour out the pain she must have been struggling with for longer than a woman should have to endure by herself. He tucked her hair over her ear and offered her a smile.

At that moment, he noticed the broken sedge grass and saw the low clearing where a wolf may have passed, venturing toward the lake. He gestured for Skylar to follow. "Give that howl one more try," he said as they walked.

Skylar let out a long howl. She was good at the vocalization.

A wolf answered almost immediately. Joe paused to study Skylar's face.

"That's her." She took off toward the lake, but she did not leave the woods, instead tracking along the edge parallel to the water. "Ahead!"

Joe followed as Skylar raced through the woods. Trees whipped at his face and shoulders, but he maintained a sure step. And then he scented the musty urine smell of wolves. It had to be the rendezvous point.

Skylar swore. He lost sight of her as she swung

around a large, ancient oak. Something was wrong. Joe swiftly rounded the tree. When he saw the scene, he called out to Skylar. She stopped just short of Stella, who sat before the immobile body of a trapped wolf.

"Aw, hell." Joe marched up to Skylar. Resisting the urge to push her aside, it took all his control to squat and hold out a hand toward Stella. "Come here, sweetie. This is not a place for you to be."

The wolf whined and crawled forward a few paces on her front legs, but she didn't seem to want to leave the trapped wolf.

A dead wolf. Thank goodness. Because much as Joe hated to lose another wolf to a trapper or poacher, the worse result would be to find the wolf still alive, suffering a slow death from what would surely be a fatal bone break or injury.

"Stella." Skylar patted her thigh and the wolf lifted her head, eyeing her person with hope. "Come to me. Let Joe take care of her."

The trap had snapped the wolf's neck. A quick death? He hoped so. And it couldn't have been in the trap long, for the insect activity was low. Just a few flies. This could have only happened within the past few hours.

"Damn poachers," Joe said curtly. "It's okay, Stella. You knew she was in trouble and you sought her out. Good girl. Now let me take care of her for you."

"Stella," Skylar said more softly.

Finally the wolf got up and approached Joe, sniffing cautiously at his outstretched fingers. He carefully slid a hand along her neck and patted her back gently. "Go to Skylar," he said. "She's worried about you."

The wolf did so, approaching Skylar with bowed head. When she got up to her and Skylar knelt, Stella bowed her head against Skylar's shoulder.

"I'm so sorry," Skylar said to the wolf. "What are we going to do about this?" she asked Joe.

"*We* are doing nothing. *You* are taking Stella home. Leave this to me."

"But I want to—"

"Go, Skylar!" The order came out with more vitriol than he intended, but it was too late to take it back, though it hurt his heart. Skylar was a member of the very family that had likely committed this atrocity. And much as he knew she was no accomplice, he couldn't move beyond that anger. "I'll carry her to my truck and turn her over to the wildlife division. They keep track of the trapped wolves in the area."

"I can help."

"You've done enough." With that, Joe rose and faced her down. Stella's ears folded back. He hated that he must appear a dominating alpha to the wolf, but he needed Skylar to just leave.

With a nod and a pat to Stella's head, Skylar rose and turned to walk away. Stella followed, glancing back frequently until the twosome landed on the lakeshore. They would follow that back to the cabin.

Joe blew out a breath. Another innocent creature's life taken for sport and profit. This had to stop. Anger coursed through his veins. He was just one man. He felt like he may never win this struggle.

Max's words echoed in his head: *You respect them, they respect you.*

He did respect them and would help them until he could do no more. Someone had to.

But was Skylar on his side or her own?

Chapter Fifteen

Joe's accusatory tone had been clear. He suspected her of involvement in the poaching. How dare he? Had he not listened to a word she'd said? She'd opened herself to him, had told him things she hadn't dared tell anyone.

Cole had told him she was the mastermind behind the poaching? Skylar would give that man a piece of her mind. And soon. He had no right to spread such lies about her.

Right now though, she wanted to get Stella home, and check her fluids and stats. She was still recovering. That she'd tracked all the way to the rendezvous site meant that she'd known about the trapped wolf. Wolves had such excellent senses of smell. Had she known Skylar would find her and rescue the wolf? Surely she had. Unfortunately, that wolf had been dead. Skylar prayed she had not suffered long after the steel trap jaws had snapped about her neck. There hadn't been noticeable signs of struggle in the dirt near where the wolf had lain. That could be a good sign.

After they reached the backyard, Stella trotted up the deck stairs and curled up in her bed.

"I'll get you something to eat," Skylar said. To Stella's sudden whine, she offered, "Without poison in it. And some fresh water, as well. No more wandering off, you got that?"

Stella lay down her head and wagged her tail.

THE TIMBER WOLF Joe had untangled from the trap and transported to the fish and game office had been tagged. He'd written down the tag ID before handing the wolf off for processing. They would check the body for its state of health, age and other important telling details that could be used in the wolf data for the state. Joe had also suggested they check for strychnine. Just an added precaution. He'd worn gloves and had been cautious to make sure the fur had not touched his skin when he'd tossed it over a shoulder to carry to the truck.

Now, back at home, after a shower to ensure no traces of contamination from the wolf might linger—he was overly cautious of poison lately—Joe slipped on some jeans and padded down to his office. He pulled up a chair behind his desk and powered up the computer. He rarely spent time in the office so it would take a few minutes for the computer to come alive. Meanwhile, he sipped his coffee and thought about how he'd left Skylar's place without a goodbye. He'd been too angry after hauling the hundred-pound dead wolf off her property. If she was involved in any way...

He didn't want to believe that. No woman who had rescued a wolf pup from a trap and made it a pet could be so cruel. And she had a naked chicken running around her property. And that crazy goat. Skylar was not inhumane.

Which meant everything she'd told him had been the truth. Cole Pruitt had lied to him. While he'd never known the man to lie, he had only known him a few years. They'd met in college and had become instant buddies. Whenever Cole had wanted to go out fishing, Joe had accompanied him. Of course, Joe did catch and release. He wasn't completely vegetarian, but he found it difficult to justify taking another being's life just to satisfy his palate. Cole had razzed him about it, going on about enjoying big steaks drowning in horseradish and butter. Joe took it all in stride. No man can change another; it was only himself he could change.

More of Max's wisdom that had crept into Joe's veins over the years.

"Max." He tapped his fingers on the desk as he thought about that buried eagle he'd found. Max had not been hiding evidence of his own foul play. "Was it the Davis family?"

Max had never mentioned anything about a run-in with Malcolm Davis or anyone else from Davis Trucking. Still, he obviously had said as much to the man Joe had spoken to on the beach. Who had found Max? Who had camped about six miles into the forest, following unmarked paths and using landmarks only experienced hikers and those who knew the land well could recognize?

Unless Max had found the bird close to the highway? No. He wouldn't have carried it all the way back to camp. Maybe?

Joe shook his head. He would never know what had gone on from the moment Max had found the bird—he needed to hear from Forensics to verify his guess it had been poisoned—until that terrible moment he had been found roadside and near death. The poor man. That was no way to die.

He checked his watch—7:30 p.m. The forensic lab might still be at it. He pressed the speed dial for them, and when it went to voice mail he clicked off. He'd call again in the morning.

The computer screen displayed a wildlife scene with a fish breaking the surface of Lake Vaillant. Joe had taken that photo himself on a cool September morning when the mosquitos had been buzzing over the water, a delicious treat for an industrious trout. He opened the state registry and typed in the wolf ID.

"The Red Seven pack," he muttered.

They were the closest pack to the area, yet still a good ten miles to the north, embedded within the Boundary Waters thick forest. If they had reason to travel south, that would land them on Skylar's property. The old rendezvous point, which was on her property, showed on a map, yet he decided it was no longer in use. Or wouldn't be, after the pack smelled the hunter and realized they'd lost one of their own. That reduced that pack to six. One alpha, two females, and he guessed the dead wolf was a lesser male. Perhaps even an omega, for the wolf had a scarred ear, showing it had either been torn in the woods or in a scrap within the pack.

Wolves showed their dominance by fighting and protecting the females. There was a definite hierarchy within the pack, and they all knew their places. But there were always the aggressive few who tried to challenge the alphas or take a female for themselves. Hell, they were constantly waiting, watching for the elders to show weakness and signs of needing to be replaced.

When he was nineteen, Joe had spent a whole year living in the Boundary Waters as part of a wildlife rescue program. It had been Max's suggestion he sign up, and despite his parents' concerns about him leaving the grid for a whole year, they'd backed him up, knowing it could help their son thrive. Joe had learned to track all kinds of animals, including cougar, elk, moose, badgers and wolves, and had learned everything he could about their ways and habitats.

A man had to abandon the industrial world, set aside his cell phone and dependence on microwaved food, and camp out in the wild to truly learn about the beautiful creatures on this earth. That summer, he'd canoed and camped through the entire Boundary Waters. And he'd been rewarded with the trust of those animals that no longer raced away when they sensed his presence. Joe knew how to tread the earth as if walking on clouds, and that silence was the only way to feel the heartbeat of the land and those animals around him.

It reminded him of another of Max's bits of wisdom. *You must hear the land. Walk upon it with reverence.* There was no way to do that with technology in hand.

Hunters—and worse, poachers—disrespected the wildlife with their entitled attitude that they had a right to take an animal for food. Some took the animals and sold them on the black market. Deer and moose antlers were sold to artisans for artwork. It was a crying shame that bald eagles were hunted for traditional Native American costumes. Even if the feathers and talons they used were treated with reverence and ritual, Joe wished it was a practice that would stop. But, despite the threat of prison or fines well into many thousands of dollars, and losing voting rights and the right to own or carry a gun, it was impossible to stop those who wished to profit from the deaths of such beautiful creatures.

Wolves had been taken off the DNR's endangered species list a few years ago, allowing licensed hunters to snag them, but they'd recently been put back on. The usual excuse for killing a wolf was that it had gone after a farmer's valued livestock. Panic was the first reaction. Guns always won over compassion or a simple understanding of animal nature.

There were many better ways to steer a wolf away from cattle and chickens, ways that were more humane than buckshot. Putting up a fence of bright red flags around the property scared the wolves away. Also, motion sensor lights did the trick, especially at night. But Joe knew many a hunter or farmer liked to claim the victory of telling others that he'd got himself a wolf the other night. Stood up to that creature and taken him down with a powerful rifle. Some even boasted about using AR rifles. The wolf didn't stand a chance against something so fast and powerful.

It broke Joe's heart. And his blood pressure always rose when he was in the presence of a poacher or when he happened upon what he'd found this afternoon. Which was why he'd taken his anger out on Skylar.

The wrong move.

His cell phone rang. It was Forensics.

"Saw your number on the missed calls," Lucy said. "I was just heading out, but decided this was important. That eagle you brought in was covered in strychnine. I was able to trace it to the poisoned eagle meat you brought in the other day. Same batch of poison."

"Really? You can determine that?"

"It was tainted with lead. Must have been stored improperly. But yes, I'm sure the source was the same. Which means somehow, the old man who handled that eagle came back from the dead to place those meat chunks you found on a lakeshore."

"You're being facetious, right?"

"I am. I think you've got a murder case on your hands, Joe."

Joe nodded. His suspicions about Max being poisoned were true. But knowing that did not make his heart whole; instead, it felt as if he'd been stabbed.

"Cash?"

"Got it. Thanks."

"I'm forwarding the toxicology report to the sheriff's department. They need this information about Max Owen's death."

"Do that. Send me a copy of it as well, please."

"Just clicked Send on your email. I'm sorry, Cash. The old man meant something to you?"

"He was a friend. Thanks, Lucy."

Joe hung up, then put his palm against his forehead. Someone had murdered Max Owen.

So the connection could be... "The sniper?" But the

trap evidence they'd found near the sniping spot had not been contaminated with poison.

So far, the common thread was the eagles.

When his phone rang, Joe thought to let it go to voice mail until he noticed the name.

He answered. "Skylar."

"I thought you might stop in before you left. Did you get the wolf and the trap?"

"I did. I've got a lot of work on this right now—"

"Right. Sorry to bother you. I just..." Her sigh echoed heavily across the phone line. "I need to tell you about Cole and me. We were distracted by looking for Stella before I could explain. Are you willing to listen?"

"Cole used to be my friend," Joe said, "but I trust you more than him. And I honestly cannot conceive of you doing such a terrible thing to innocent animals."

"Sure felt like you were mad at me for something earlier."

Joe exhaled. "Sorry about that. I get angry when I find a dead animal in a trap. I took that anger out on you."

"I can understand, with the investigation."

"Tell me the real story about you and Cole. Please?"

"I can't believe he would say that it was me involved in the poaching. No, actually I do believe it. That man is a duplicitous charmer who hisses when he slides through the grass. I left him at the altar, Joe. I had just found out Cole was friends with Malcolm, and had been doing some work for him. That day I went to Cole's place and I found snares and traps in his shed. And there was a bag of eagle feathers tucked in a drawer in his bedroom. He lied to you. And I don't know why he would want you to believe I'm involved, but I'm not. I could never."

She gasped. Was she fighting tears?

He wished he could pull her to him and tell her she was going to be all right. He hated knowing she had been hurt and that Cole was the reason for it. But right now he needed the distance. Because his heart hurt desperately for the loss of a good friend.

"You did the right thing," he said, "even though it might not feel like it. And you may feel alone and scared, but trust me, Skylar, I'm here for you."

"Are you really?"

"I am. Promise. I won't let Cole Pruitt come near you. Or Malcolm Davis. Is he the one you suspect shot at you? And the one who poisoned Stella?"

"I'm not sure it was Malcolm. He's got others who do his dirty work. Like the guy in the warehouse who threatened me."

"Think you could positively identify the man if I had you look through some mug shots?"

"I'm sure I could, but… I don't know."

"I might not even need a mug shot. I'm on the Davis Trucking website right now. There's an employee roster and some headshots. You said he was a redhead? There's a couple redheads," Joe said as he moved the mouse over the page. "Can you go online and take a look?"

"I can do that. But…will Malcolm find out?"

"If you can identify the man who threatened you, no one will need to know it was you. But catching them with evidence in hand is key. Have you ever seen them setting the traps on your property?"

"No. And I'm not sure they're aware of the property boundaries, because it's always close to the edge of where my land meets the DNR-owned land. They need a map."

Joe sighed. "They need to stop."

"Even better."

"You sure you saw eagle feathers in Cole's possession?"

"Yes."

Joe exhaled.

She sighed. "When will you stop by next?"

"How about in the morning? I have a lot of work to do right now. How's Stella doing?"

"She's good. Loping about this evening and playing with Becky. But she's suspicious of the chopped turkey I offered her. Might have to stick with kibble for a while until she trusts meat again."

"Poor girl. Can I...?" Joe rubbed his jaw. Dare he push it between the two of them? She'd confessed she wasn't involved, and he believed her 100 percent. Now, to make up to her for his harsh treatment earlier. "Can I bring lunch by tomorrow? Maybe we can have a picnic out on your deck?"

"That sounds wonderful. I'll make something sweet for dessert."

"Sounds like a plan. Don't forget to take a look at the trucking website."

"Will do. Talk to you tomorrow, Joe."

Joe hung up and smiled. That call had improved his

mood. But only until he eyed the laptop screen again. Foremost on his agenda was learning who was poaching eagles and handling strychnine. He didn't have probable cause to search Davis Trucking. Not until he could place one of their employees at the scene of the sniper shooting.

There were two men with red hair shown on the roster. Could be many other employees who didn't have their photos on the site. And there were a couple shots in black-and-white, so no way to determine hair color. He'd wait and see if Skylar recognized one of them. Then he'd have grounds to bring him in for questioning. Because threatening a woman with a rifle? That was criminal assault.

With luck, he'd be able to secure an arrest warrant by tomorrow afternoon.

Chapter Sixteen

Skylar said goodbye to the owner of the farm-supply store. He'd sold her some clinical supplies and IV fluids that he ordered from a veterinary site. Stella was out of the woods medically, but Skylar wanted to replenish her stock. After leaving the store, she strolled down the sidewalk with the small box under an arm, nodding to a pair of elderly women who smiled bright, wrinkled grins.

Passing a big black four-by-four truck, she suddenly realized it was Malcolm's and paused just by the passenger door. She had no intention of talking to him. What was he in town for?

Across the street sat the café, and next to that a small office that rented to a variety of mobile businesses, including a tax accountant and a lawyer.

Skylar sucked in her lower lip. A lawyer. That made sense. Malcolm must have reason to employ all sorts of legal help. But a traveling lawyer? Good thing he'd never signed on with her dad's lawyer. Of course, she figured that could have been a conflict of interest on the solicitor's part.

Her mom owned half the land. She was still processing that information. And did she want to find her?

Part of her said, *Hell no*. But that part was the pre-teen girl who had wanted to run after Dorothy and beg her to explain herself.

Now she didn't want to think about it. She couldn't. Not with Malcolm and his crew breathing down her neck.

She glanced inside the truck. A brown file folder and some mail were strewn on the passenger seat. As well, a flyer for a local powwow. Why was Malcolm going to a powwow, or even interested in one?

And then it hit her. Hard.

She had to tell Joe.

SINGING ALONG TO Lynyrd Skynard's "Freebird," Joe navigated his way back toward Checker Hill. He'd just come off the lake. A group of five boats had been reported playing loud music, and girls were flipping up their T-shirts to expose themselves to passing boaters. Kids and booze and boats never mixed. Joe had been flashed three times in the process of issuing them tickets and following them inland to dock their boats. He hadn't made any arrests, but a stern warning, and the mention that he knew more than a few of their parents, had been taken seriously.

Now he intended to pick up some groceries for the meal he'd promised Skylar. He wasn't going to get prepared foods from the deli section. No, he had a few specialties he could make. She would get a taste of his macaroni special.

He checked his reflection in the rearview mirror. Should have shaved this morning. He was looking a little rough. Probably needed a haircut, too. His bangs hung in his eyes. He rubbed his stubble, thinking maybe he should try for a full beard like his brother Justin.

A beat-up Ford that had once been red and was now pushing for pink passed him in the other lane, going the opposite direction. Too late, Joe raised a hand to wave. That had been Skylar. She must be headed home from the errands she'd mentioned. They'd just passed, like two ships. The thought made him smile. He planned a docking this evening.

Man, did that sound corny.

Another car passed him, going well over the speed limit. A determined red sedan, which suddenly swerved out of its lane.

Joe touched the radio intercom to get through to county dispatch.

He didn't hear the sound of impact, but Joe saw the collision in his rearview mirror.

Chapter Seventeen

Joe slammed on the brakes, steering to the gravel road-side. Half a mile down the road, Skylar's truck sat in the ditch. The red car had continued driving.

He turned the truck around, switching on the police flashers as he did so. He waited for Dispatch to respond while he drove, keeping his eyes pinned on the red sedan, which quickly distanced itself from the scene of the accident. Damn it, he should have gotten a license plate.

Pulling up behind Skylar's truck, he saw motion behind the wheel. That meant she was alive. Looked like the driver of the red car had nudged her rear bumper, forcing her into the ditch.

Dispatch prompted him, and he realized she'd questioned him twice already.

"I've got a car run off the road on County Road 7. I'm getting out to investigate now. If there's a patrol in the area, the perp was driving a red two-door Monte Carlo. I didn't take note of the plates. I'll pursue after checking on the driver, who was run into the ditch."

"I'll send an ambulance," Dispatch said.

Joe knew Skylar would protest if she wasn't hurt too badly, but it was standard procedure.

"Thanks."

He got out of his truck and raced up to Skylar's vehicle. The front end had hit a broken telephone pole. Long out of use and rotting, the foot-wide base was still intact. It had served to stop the truck from sinking into the water, which Joe estimated to be about a foot deep. The front of the engine was crushed in. The vehicle was totaled.

He pulled open the driver's door and Skylar blinked at him. Her forehead bled, and her lower lip wobbled.

"I'm here," he said. "I saw you pass me. Did you see who was driving the red car?"

She shook her head and held out her arms. He stepped up to help her down.

"How badly are you hurt?" he asked.

"Just shaken. My head hit the steering wheel because I was turning the radio dial when he slammed into me. I lost control, and the truck veered sharply." She clutched his arms and stepped onto the side runner.

Joe decided to sweep her into his arms. She didn't protest, which meant she had been shaken. He carried her back to his truck and gently set her down near the hood. Brushing aside her blond hair, he inspected the cut on her temple. It wasn't deep, more like a bruise. But she could have whiplash or other internal injuries.

"Dispatch called for an ambulance."

"Oh no, Joe. I'm fine."

She wobbled, and he caught her against him. He wrapped his arms around her and pressed his cheek to the crown of her head. She shook in his arms. He wasn't sure what he would have done if she'd been seriously injured, or worse.

More than anything, he wanted to go after the driver who had done this to her. It hadn't been an accident. The car had been swerving, which led Joe to believe the driver had been under the influence. Yet that driver had been clearheaded enough to have purposely gone after Skylar, accelerating until he'd been able to bump her into the ditch.

"Your ribs or anything else hurt?" he asked. Her body felt warm against his, but her shivers troubled him. She could go into shock if he didn't keep her calm and comfortable.

She shook her head. "I feel like you've been rescuing me a lot lately."

"I did tell you I'd be there for you. I just wish I could have stopped this before it happened. I wonder who that was. If I get going, I could probably track him down."

"Then you should go."

"I can't leave you alone."

"You said an ambulance was on the way. I'm going to be fine, Joe. I don't even want to go to the hospital."

"They'll take you to the clinic in town. Let me stay until the ambulance arrives, Skylar."

She shook her head. "No. Go. I want you to find whoever did this."

"You sure? Let me help you to the back of your truck to wait…"

An ambulance siren sounded miles away.

"The cavalry is on their way," Skylar said. "You

take off. It's only been a few minutes. You can still catch him."

"You're sure it was a him?"

"I don't know. I wasn't paying attention to the car coming up behind me, then—crash!"

He pulled her close again and pressed his lips to her head. Her hair smelled sweet, and her body melded against his. He didn't want to let her go, but if he didn't, whoever had done this might get away with the crime.

"All right." He forced himself to walk away from the shaken woman. As he pulled out from the shoulder, the ambulance drove up.

The EMT driver rolled down his window. "Hit-and-run?"

"Yes. She's stable. I want to pursue."

"Go for it. We've got it from here."

IT TOOK FIVE minutes to catch up on the two-lane county road. It was normally a highly traveled road, but not so much at this time of day. That was one thing to be thankful for, because others might have gotten in the driver's way and the results could have been far worse. The red sedan led Joe all the way to the next town, fifteen miles east, and into the weedy lot of an empty fairgrounds. The driver parked at an angle in the big lot, then the door opened and out tumbled the driver. Cole Pruitt scrambled across the tarmac, slipping and stumbling as he landed on the grassy lawn.

Checking that the gun was holstered at his hip with a firm clasp, Joe ran after the man, seriously hoping he would not have to draw on him. The last thing he expected was to chase down a friend after he'd been involved in a hit-and-run.

"Cole!"

Cole stumbled again, and as he looked over his shoulder, his feet tangled and he went down, groaning, cursing and kicking at the air in his frustration.

Joe could smell the whiskey when he got close. Whatever the hell was going on with this man, he wanted to know. Because he had done a drastic one-eighty since he and Joe had been friends.

"You're under arrest, Cole," Joe said as he knelt. With a simple shove, he managed to get the grumbling drunk onto his stomach. He secured one wrist and slapped handcuffs onto him. "For driving under the influence, and the hit-and-run of Skylar Davis."

He turned Cole over and he muttered, "Screw you, Cash."

The man passed out, mouth open and legs sprawled.

Joe hated when the perp passed out. He'd need another officer to help him get Cole into the car and transported to the county jail. With a shake of his head, he wandered back to his truck and called Dispatch. Help would arrive in fifteen minutes.

All he could think about was that he'd had to leave Skylar, injured, by the side of the road. And that thought brought up the image of Max also lying roadside, obviously seeking help. What had his last moments been like, to have possibly known he'd been poisoned with nothing he could do about it? Whoever had left that eagle near his property was responsible. And while Forensics had not been able to get fingerprints or human

DNA evidence from the bird, Joe knew all paths had to lead to Davis Trucking.

And if Cole Pruitt was working for Malcolm Davis, then Joe was not going to relent until Cole given him answers.

Chapter Eighteen

Joe pulled up to the county hospital and ran inside. He'd told Skylar they would take her to a clinic, but he'd known better. She probably had, too. The clinic closed early and didn't have emergency services. He veered down the hallway in the direction of the ER. It was nearing supper time, and the waiting room was packed with people, from babies to geriatrics. It had only been a few weeks since he'd last been here, looking for Max, hoping he was alive…

He stopped at the admissions desk. "Skylar Davis. She was brought in via ambulance. I'm with the DNR and was first on scene. And I'm a friend. Which room is she in?"

"Number eleven." The redhead behind the desk, with bespangled glasses perched at the end of her nose, pressed a button. To the right, a security door opened.

Joe ran for the door. Room eleven was around the corner. He soared in through the curtained divide to find Skylar sitting on the edge of the bed, her forehead bandaged, sipping juice from a tiny, brightly colored box.

"I tried to get here as fast as I could," Joe said. "What's the damage?"

"Just a cut and possible concussion. I'm supposed to have someone checking on me through the night, but I told them I'm okay to go home on my own."

"No, you're not. They give those orders for a reason. I'll take you home and watch you through the night."

Skylar's eyebrow lifted suggestively. "I think I can get behind that."

"You see? You're not thinking straight now, inviting strange men home with you."

"You do have your strange moments, Joe." She waggled the juice box. "Want a sip?"

"No, I'll let you have all that goofy grape for yourself. When will they release you?"

"The doctors are currently weighing my request to leave on my own, so I expect as soon as we can flag one down and tell them I now have a babysitter, I'll be good to go. I'm starving."

"Sorry, I was supposed to bring something to eat. And for lunch. We both got sidetracked. We can pick up something on the way home. Dairy Queen has a special."

"I'm in. As long as I can also get a chocolate malt. And not one of those impostor shakes. It's gotta have real malt in it."

"Deal." He sat on the bed beside her and studied the bandage. It was small, with no signs of blood seeping through. "Did they do a brain scan?"

"What for?"

"To make sure everything's still in there."

"Seriously?"

He let a smile escape. "I'm kidding. You're the smartest woman I know, and still could be."

"*Could* be?"

"Well, when you get your brains joggled…" He let that hang, hoping she'd take it for the joke he meant it to be.

"I may have lost an IQ point or two. I can deal with that. But more important, is my truck totaled?"

"I'd make a guess it is. The engine was crushed. You're lucky you weren't seriously hurt. God, I'm so glad you're okay, Skylar."

He hugged her from the side. She was solid and real and not dead. It could have gone any way when she'd hit that telephone pole. A little to the left, and the pole could have sheered through the front of the vehicle and cut into the cab where she was sitting. Or had she not been wearing a seat belt, she could have flown through the windshield.

But she was safe. And mostly sound.

"Did you catch the guy?" she asked from within his arms.

"Yes, and uh…you sure you didn't recognize that car?"

"I didn't. I mean, I remember it was red, but everything happened so quickly. Why should I have recognized it? Who was it, Joe?"

"It was Cole Pruitt."

He felt her tense up in his arms and released his grip, allowing her to sit back. A deep exhale was followed by her shivery release of breath. "Cole? Really?"

"He was drunk. But that's no excuse. He knew exactly what he was doing. I arrested him and put him in the county jail. I plan to talk to him in the morning after he's sobered up. After all you've told me, there could be a lot of reasons he went after you, but I've never known the man to be the sort who would want to harm a person because they brushed him off or…left him at the altar."

"It's the poaching," Skylar said on a whisper. She glanced around. The ER was a hum of buzzers and alarms, and a baby wailed relentlessly a few rooms down. They were secluded in the little room, and no one paid them any mind. "I feel like there's something bigger going on, Joe. And Cole is involved. And whatever is going on, I think he's in over his head. He never drinks enough to get drunk. He likes his beer, but—"

"The breathalyzer showed he was well over the legal limit. He'd been drinking whiskey."

"That's his kryptonite. He usually walks a wide circle around that stuff. I know, because I have offered him brandy and he's refused that, as well, saying the hard stuff never agrees with him."

"I know the same about him. So why is he suddenly drinking and acting out of character? You talk to him about any of your suspicions?"

"Haven't talked to him for two months, since I walked—or rather, ran—away from the altar. Don't want to talk to him. But—" she winced, touching her forehead "—do you think I should?"

"Absolutely not. Let me handle this. I think you're right. There's something bigger going on, and I'm just starting to touch the edges of it all. The poaching is bad enough, but—did you ever hear Cole mention poison?"

"Never. You don't think he poisoned Stella? The two of them never got along, but I don't think…" Her shoulders slumped. "Though if he can bring himself to poach animals, then anything is possible. And if Malcolm ordered him to do so…" She sighed. "I really hate to believe that about him."

"Yeah, I'm not so sure he would do that to Stella." Or Max, for that matter. That would be premeditated murder. No, Joe wouldn't put Cole in that category. But— "What about those eagles you mentioned? You saw feathers in Cole's residence. Ever see anything else?"

"No. But if he's involved with my uncle, then I wouldn't put it past him. Those feathers though. He had a couple of them in a plastic baggie."

"They sell for big bucks on the black market. Tribes buy them for their costumes."

"That's it!"

"What's it?"

Skylar put a finger to her lips.

The doctor, a tall, thin woman with a swinging blond ponytail and pink running shoes to match her scrubs, breezed in. She flashed a penlight at both of Skylar's pupils.

"Looks good. I would prefer you remain here for the night, Miss Davis, if you don't have anyone to take you home—"

"I got that covered," Joe offered. "I'll be her watchdog."

The doctor's smile grew knowingly bright, but she

didn't wink. Thank goodness. "Great. I'll put in for her release and send you home with instructions for her care through the night. I'll have a nurse come in and wheel you out, Miss Davis."

"Wheel me out?"

"Take advantage of it," Joe said. "How often is it you get the five-star treatment? I'll run out and pull the truck up to the door." He kissed her forehead. "Be right back."

THEY DIDN'T SPEAK until they'd gotten out of the Ford at the DQ and sat on the faded blue plastic benches at the far side of the outdoor court.

"So." Joe took a bite of his salad and then a sip of the Cherry Slush.

"So?"

"You had a eureka moment back in the ER."

"Right. Joe." She laid a hand over his. "It hit me when you mentioned Native Americans buying feathers for their costumes. I walked by Malcolm's truck today when I was in town."

"And?"

"I looked inside and saw a flyer, and couldn't figure why he'd be interested in something like that. I mean, he's the last man I'd even expect to care about Native American culture, let alone want to attend a powwow."

"A powwow?"

"That's what the flyer was for. There's one next month up at the Grand Portage Reservation."

"Interesting."

"You think he sells eagle parts to them?"

"Not out in the open. But that would certainly be the place to make connections. Build up a clientele. Thanks, Skylar."

"Guess my brain didn't get as joggled as we thought."

"You're still not getting rid of the babysitter."

"Wouldn't dream of trying."

NIGHT SOFTENED THE sky to a chrome gray with dashes of lilac edging the few clouds. Mosquitos buzzed about the lights on the deck. Chickens hushed out low, contented noises from the henhouse. Wet bark and moss perfumed the air. The day had been too long. Skylar should go immediately to bed. But where to put Joe? On the couch? In her bed?

Because despite what was going on in her life, she really needed to be held right now. To know that she was wanted, and yes, to feel sexy and attractive. She hadn't anticipated a moment like this—Joe having to spend the night—but a woman would be a fool not to entertain the notion of fooling around. Really, she did need to be checked on frequently. What better plan than to allow the man close access to her?

Joe closed the front door and called out to Stella, who came bounding through the pet door connected to the patio. The wolf bypassed Skylar and went straight for Joe, greeting him with a slobbery kiss and knocking him to the floor, where he let her shower him with all the love she could manage.

"I'm a little jealous," Skylar said. More than a little, something she'd never admit to Joe. "But she is a smart wolf. She knows a good man when she sees one."

The behavior she exhibited with Joe was so un-wolf-like that Skylar almost felt embarrassed for her.

"I surrender!" Joe called out. The man stretched out his arms across the floor, and Stella stopped licking his face and sat alert beside him. "She's recovered one hundred percent," he announced.

"Yes, makes me glad."

"You going to shower and head to bed? The instructions the doctor gave me say I have to wake you up every two to three hours."

She was not going to stop a man from touching her every few hours. "I'll let you do what you gotta do. As for a shower..." She walked over to him and knelt on the floor. He still lay on his back. Stella looked to her curiously. The wolf's ears rotated, and she tilted her head. "You want to join me?"

Joe sat up abruptly, catching his elbows on the floor. He narrowed his gaze on her. "Is this the part where you have crazy thoughts because of the bump on your head?"

"Do you think taking a shower with me sounds crazy?"

"Hell, Skylar, that sounds like a dream, but..."

She bent down and kissed him. It was a firm and long kiss. Gliding her hand down his chest, she tucked a finger along the buttons and touched hot skin. She wanted him. Now.

No strings. She needed this.

"I want you, Joe," she said, and kissed his cheek, then moved her lips along his jaw and up to tongue at his earlobe. "Don't you want me?"

"I do. But I don't want to take advantage of a woman who's been injured and her brain—"

Another kiss was necessary to stop his ridiculous protest.

"Don't say no to me this time, Joe. Neither one of us has been drinking."

"I am completely sober. But you—"

She kissed him again to silence his protest. He settled into the kiss and soon spread a hand up her back to pull her closer.

"I am of sound mind and body right now," she said.

"You most certainly are."

"I'm going to fill Stella's water dish and make sure she's got kibble," she said as she sat up. "If I don't hear that shower running in a few minutes, I'm going to think you're not interested in me at all."

Joe stood and started toward the bathroom. "I can take an order!" he called.

Skylar laughed and ruffled Stella's fur. "Come on, Stella."

Chapter Nineteen

Water slicked over Skylar's skin and under Joe's palm as he glided it from her neck, down her chest and over her full breasts. He bowed to kiss each one and then lave the nipples. The night had taken an unexpected turn, but he was no man to argue. The two of them standing together, naked, in the shower, might be because of her head injury, but he didn't think so. Skylar was smart, and as she'd said, neither one of them were drunk. This time.

He'd regretted missing this opportunity years ago. He would never regret again when it came to her. This could very well be a one-night stand, which would challenge his wanting heart. But, right now, all that mattered was the two of them, skin against skin. Heartbeats racing. Moans mingling.

He kissed her mouth and pulled her in close. Her slick skin glided under his touch. His erection had achieved steel status, but they hadn't gone beyond kissing. He couldn't wait much longer and, to judge by her moans, neither could she.

"We're clean," he suddenly said. "Race you to the bed?"

"I get a head start."

"What?"

"I *am* injured."

"Fair enough." He switched off the shower, and Skylar pulled down a towel and pressed it to her face. When she pulled it away, he kissed her forehead and then licked the water droplets.

"You sure you're up for this?" he asked.

"Oh, Joe, are you sure *you* are?" She teased her fingers down his wet abdomen and then gripped his cock.

He winced at the teasing squeeze, and nodded. The woman was in control, and he didn't mind that one bit. "You'd better get going," he said. "I'll be right behind you."

He toweled off after she left the bathroom. He heard her talk to Stella, and the wolf pattered down the hallway toward the back of the house. Had Skylar consigned the wolf to the deck? She must be really serious about this.

And he was no man to keep her waiting.

Wrapping the towel about his hips, Joe wandered down the hardwood-floored hallway and into the bedroom. He found Skylar lying on the white sheets on her stomach, her toes entwined with one another. She crooked a finger into a "come here" gesture. When he got to the end of the bed, she put up her palm and said, "Wait."

He held the towel and did as he was told.

"One night," she said. "No strings."

Every bone in his body tried to get Joe to protest that statement. He wanted strings. He wanted complications.

He wanted Skylar. All the time, every time. And yet... she had just gotten out of a bad relationship. He was willing to play the game her way. Because he wasn't willing to lose her a second time.

"Agreed," he said. He dropped the towel and took some pride in the slow glide of Skylar's tongue along her lower lip as she took him in.

Joe sipped coffee while Stella lapped at water in her bowl, a noisy undertaking on her part. Skylar sat across the kitchen table from him, his green cotton shirt the only thing she wore—she hadn't buttoned it. Her long hair spilled like sun-toasted wheat over her shoulders. And the tiny mole that sat high on her left breast peeked out at him. She was gorgeous. And he would give everything he owned to go back to the bedroom and spend the rest of the day snuggling and making love with her.

But the very reason they had come together was because of a sinister evil that surrounded the Davis land and threatened Skylar's safety. He wasn't about to let that simmer reach a boil.

He set down his coffee mug and pulled out his cell phone from his back jeans pocket. He'd finish dressing when Skylar decided to hand over his shirt. Damn, it looked good on her.

"Business so soon?" she asked, catching her cheek against the heel of her palm as she leaned forward onto the table.

"Yes. I finally got a copy of the waiting list that tribes sign up for to receive eagle parts. Apparently, the wait is long."

"Thus, the black market."

"You know about that?"

"I know about a lot of things I'd rather be oblivious to. I remember years ago my dad found a dead eagle on our land. Hadn't been poached. Looked like it had a run-in with something with teeth. Anyway, he was going to bury it, but before he did, he carefully removed the feathers. Told me he had a friend on the Fond du Lac Reservation who could use them. That's when he told me about the illegal sale of those feathers, and all the other animal parts a person never imagines would bring in a price. Like bear gall bladders. They import those to Asia for medicines. It's nuts."

"Sometimes man can be ignorantly cruel." Joe scrolled through the list. Max's tribe was at the bottom. A long wait.

"So, Cole is stewing in the county jail right now?"

Joe set his phone on the table. "I wouldn't mind letting him sit there all day, but I've got to move while opportunity presents itself."

Joe wandered over, and when Skylar turned he pulled her into his arms. "But you *were* going to make the leap with Cole."

She looked aside. "I'd rather not discuss that."

"I know I don't have a right to ask. And I know you asked for the no-strings deal last night. But I'm hoping what's going on between us right now is going to become something much more…"

"Long lasting?" She bowed her head against his shoulder, then looked up, offering a shrug. "I'm *not* thinking about marriage."

"Don't worry. I haven't picked out a little pink house. Yet. But I do want to know about you and Cole. Why you decided that marriage was right between you two."

"I get that. And I'll tell you. Someday. But right now, things are too fresh, and we're only just getting to know one another again. Can we take it slow?"

"I can work with that. But with everything that's going on right now, I don't want you going near Cole or talking to him, understand?"

"I might be able to get some answers from him if you let me talk to him. Maybe I can accompany you on the interrogation?"

"That's my job, Skylar. A job that demands my attention right now. I'm heading in to town. That is, if I can get my shirt back."

She ran her palms across his bare chest. "You don't think the fish and game department will appreciate you in the buff? I know you were on the county calender a few years ago because it was right before Cole and I—"

Joe winced. Right before she and Cole got together. He didn't need the reminder.

Yeah, he'd posed for a local charity calendar. So had his brother Jason. They'd oiled up their abs and biceps, and had performed their best beefcake impressions. For a good cause. All proceeds were donated to a local camp for disabled children. Their mom had bought a hundred copies and was always giving them out to friends and bragging about her handsome sons.

"Yeah, but we were talking about Cole and you," he said. "Shirt?"

She started to shrug off his shirt, which revealed

her bare shoulders and arms and then— Mercy, her breasts were high and full. Joe bowed to kiss each one as he caught the shirt when it slipped off her hands. She moaned sweetly and tilted her shoulders back.

"Sure you want to leave so fast?" she asked.

"Nope. But yes, I have to. Not going to be easy." He moved his kisses up along her neck and jaw and landed on her mouth for a warm, long, delving dive into her sweetness. "If I don't go now, I won't be able to walk into the office without advertising."

Skylar squeezed her palms over his hard-on. "I can take care of that problem."

"You tempt me." And he could make it a quickie…

From behind them, Stella yipped softly and then performed a playful pounce.

"She doesn't have the patience to watch her person get tangled with another person this morning," Joe said. He kissed Skylar once more, then slid his shirt on and buttoned it. "I'll give you a call this afternoon."

"I'll be waiting."

He smiled as he headed toward the door. A beautiful woman waiting on him? He could get used to this.

Chapter Twenty

Cole Pruitt had a manner about him that Joe had not previously found annoying. Was it his venture into hard alcohol? Something had changed the man from fun loving and a little goofy to...this. The man sat across a steel table from Joe, hands folded on it, gray eyes holding Joe's and a smirk crimping the corner of his mouth. Cole had no right to be cocky after what he'd done to Skylar yesterday.

"So you're telling me you didn't purposely run Skylar Davis off County Road 7 yesterday afternoon at 1:45 p.m.?" Joe stated for the recording.

Cole shook his head. "Nope. I was drunk, man. I admit that. You know it. Charge me with drunk driving. But I did not go after Skylar and force her into the ditch."

Joe sat back on the uncomfortable folding chair, spreading his legs and hitching his thumbs at his belt loops. Behind him, on the other side of the two-way glass, sat Brent Kofax. He hadn't insisted on sitting in on the interrogation. Wasn't necessary. Joe had all the qualifications of a police officer and had done many an interrogation before. But should he decide to charge Cole with anything it would be through the county, and the guy was already assisting with the investigation.

It was all he could do right now *not* to punch the smirk from Cole's face. They used to spar with each other, Muay Thai style, so he knew the man could hold his own against him. Until Skylar had told him the truth about the wedding being off, and Cole's lie about her introducing him to Malcolm Davis, Joe had had no reason to hate the man. Dislike, sure. The man had won the girl. Though at the time, Joe had not pinned *purposeful stealing of the girl* on Cole. He'd known his friend had gotten lucky and asked Skylar out when she was available.

Not that Cole should have ever asked her out. He'd known how Joe had felt about her. But—hell, he was over giving the man a get-out-of-jail-free card. He was an asshole, through and through.

"Good thing you were there to rescue her, eh?" Cole shot across the table. He rapped the table. "When do you cut me loose? I suppose I gotta pay bail, show up in court—"

"You're not going anywhere until I learn everything about Malcolm Davis and your involvement with the family's criminal pursuits."

Cole snickered and gathered his hands in his lap. "I suppose Skylar wants you to believe she was the one to leave me at the altar?"

"Skylar has nothing to do with whatever it is you've been doing for Malcolm Davis. And you know it." Joe held the man's gaze until he finally glanced away, tilted his head and nodded, as if to say, *Very well.*

"They're a tough family," Cole said quietly. "And that's all I can say."

Because he knew that if he talked, he'd be punished by that tough family? Likely. The man had refused a lawyer sitting in on this interrogation. Probably shouldn't have.

Just the thought of what Malcolm Davis was involved in made Joe's skin crawl. And that was merely poaching and some minor assault arrests attributed to a few of his truckers. Could they possibly be connected to Max's murder?

"Do you want to be released?" Joe asked. "I can make sure you spend some time in county jail for reckless endangerment and leaving the scene of an accident, in addition to the DUI."

"Might be safer here," Cole muttered. Then he lifted his chin and looked Joe straight on. "I'm not telling you anything. You're not a real cop."

"My badge says I am. I was trained as a peace officer before going on to train for the DNR. I have all the abilities and legal powers of any other law enforcement officer. And you know that."

Cole curled up his top lip in disgust and looked aside, before finally announcing, "I'll only talk to Skylar."

"Skylar doesn't work for the county. And I'm the one doing the interrogation. It's me or nothing."

Cole shrugged and crossed his arms over his chest. "Then I'll take nothing."

Joe lunged across the table and gripped the man's

shirt, but just as quickly, he remembered he was being recorded. He released Cole and kicked aside the chair he'd been sitting on, then wandered along the back of the room where two-way glass was framed.

Joe ran through his options. He would not allow Cole within shouting distance of Skylar, that was for sure. He could lock him up for a while, but he'd have to charge him, and that risked sending out a smoke signal to the Davis family. If he were to get the sneak on Malcolm Davis, he needed to keep Cole's incarceration hush-hush right now. It was easy enough to hide illegal animal parts and to cover up any other crimes before a warrant could be drawn up to search the place.

"I'll tell Skylar everything," Cole offered. He nodded at Joe. "Nice talking to you, man. Now bring me back to my cell."

Joe knocked on the glass. Brent alerted the guard outside in the hallway. The door opened.

"Take him back to a cell," Joe said.

While Cole was escorted out by the guard, Joe rubbed his jaw and banged the table with a fist. Cole knew something. And the only way to get it out of him was by letting him talk to Skylar.

WHILE AT THE local police department, Joe commandeered a computer and tapped into their database. Through that he was able to view local businesses and check their employee rosters, if listed—companies were not required to release employee records. Privacy acts, and all that. But nowadays most employees signed a release protection form that allowed their information to be accessed by police and FBI if they were suspected of a crime. Only a few employees were listed on the Davis Trucking roster that had previously been released. From there, Joe cross-checked the names to police sheets, to see if they had arrests.

After an hour of work, he ended up with two employees listed as former military. One had served as a sniper with the army during the Gulf War: Reginald Marshall. And he was a redhead. His rap sheet was short, but it listed poaching and domestic violence. No DUIs, but Joe tended to assume alcohol was involved when a man beat his wife.

All of Reginald's vehicle registrations were up-to-date, and he'd applied for a building permit for a shed on his land last year. Joe couldn't come up with a reason to apply for a warrant, but he intended to find the guy and ask him some questions. Starting with where he had been the night Skylar had been shot at. If he couldn't offer an alibi, Joe would bring him in for further questioning.

His cell phone rang, and Joe sat back in the office chair to answer. His brother Jason announced he was calling from the back of a pickup truck filled with manure. He was helping a local family get an overturned truck out of the ditch before all their precious manure melded with the rain-soaked ground. He was literally up to his knees in bullshit. But between days like that and a rare moment he actually got to do real police work, his brother was happy as a camper surrounded by singing squirrels.

"Did she say yes?" Joe asked as he sorted through

his notes in the notebook he always carried with him. He'd made a diagram of all the names of the Davis family and their petty crimes. Every single one had at least two poaching offenses. Malcolm was strangely clean.

He penciled in Reginald Marshall's name on the list.

"Of course she did," Jason said. "We're getting hitched in January."

"January?"

"I convinced her since we met in that brutal month, it was only fitting we seal the deal the same month. But she got to pick the location, so we're going to say 'I do' in France. She calls it a destination wedding."

Joe rubbed his temple. He'd never been out of the country, unlike his brother, who was former CIA and had spent years traveling the globe. The idea of visiting France appealed. Of course, Jason was overlooking one key issue.

"Mom will never get on a plane," he said. Indeed, their mother was deathly afraid of flying, and had not once in her fifty-eight years set foot off the ground for more than a leap or a rotation around the Ferris wheel.

"I know. You have to help me with that one, bro. You're the one she can't say no to."

That was true.

"I'll see what I can do." Joe rapped his notes with the end of a pen. "So tell me more about sniping for the military. Could a man hit a target three-quarters of a mile away?"

"With ease. I've made the hit three miles away."

"Nice."

"I am a talented man. What kind of rifle?"

"Shells are Lapua. Forensics guesses the gun is the same make."

"Nice weapon. If the perp had been overseas, he'd have opportunity to run into something like that and possibly use it in operations. Didn't you say you were looking at a specific family involved in the poaching?"

"Malcolm Davis, who heads Davis Trucking."

"I've heard of that guy. Runs a not-so-clean operation. But we can never pin anything on him directly. Couple of his guys have been arrested for assault."

"And poaching and drunk driving," Joe said. "I think they're selling eagle parts."

"Big business, that. All across the US. Would be easy to move around with a trucking company. They know how to hide things at border checks and weigh stations."

Joe sat back and squeezed his eyelids tight. "Malcolm has got two employees who are former military. One was a sniper. I need to start matching employees with arrest records and trucking schedules. I have to talk to Cole Pruitt again. He's working with Davis, but he's keeping his mouth shut."

"Isn't that the guy—"

"Yeah, whatever. She didn't marry him."

"Skylar was her name, wasn't it?"

Joe nodded, but smiled to himself. He had woken in Skylar's bed this morning. And if things went well, their relationship would only grow.

"Skylar Davis," Jason said firmly. "Is that the same family?"

"It's her uncle. She's not involved. But they're trying to make it look like she is. That is, when they're not threatening her. Or poisoning her wolf."

"Sounds like you've got your hands full, bro."

"This started out as simply tracking local poachers, and then when Max died…"

"Who's Max?"

Joe had never told his family about Max Owen. He'd let them believe that when their lost boy had found his way out of the forest after three days, it had been the wolves who'd led him home. As they had. But only by Max's direction. It was strange enough to see one's son being led home by wolves, but to know he'd spent days with a stranger alone in the forest? At the time, Joe had had the sense not to upset his parents even more. As well, he'd wanted to keep Max a secret because he had wanted him to have his freedom, and not be bothered by local reporters or even the police.

Max hadn't harmed him in any way. He'd only opened Joe's heart and mind to the world.

"Guy I used to know," Joe said. "He was poisoned a few weeks ago. Coroner ruled it accidental, but I think it's related to the poaching, and was purposeful. Been finding the same poison running through this whole investigation."

"Why would someone poison an old man?"

"Exactly."

"He had to have known something. You got help with this, Joseph?"

"Brent Kofax, with the sheriff's department, is my backup."

"He's a good cop. Well, give me a holler if you want me to drive up there. I'm only a half hour away."

"I will. But I wouldn't want to take you away from all that important bullshit."

Jason laughed.

"I'm good for now," Joe said. "But who's the brother who's doing actual police work now, eh?"

"I think that's Justin," Jason deadpanned.

Joe sighed. He knew it was a joke, but it still hurt that his brother could not accept that he was doing real police work.

"How's he doing with the private investigation work?" Joe asked. "I haven't talked to him for weeks."

"Ah, you know. He's adjusting. That brain injury did a number on him. He looks and acts normal, but I think some things give him trouble."

Joe knew Justin took medication, which any man who had been shot through the brain would. "He wants to be back in a patrol car."

"He wants that position with the FBI that he missed out on because of the damned bullet."

"Yeah, he's had a tough year. I'll make a point of visiting him soon."

"This weekend! See you at Mom and Dad's this Saturday?" Jason said. "Dad's birthday, remember?"

He had forgotten. That was four days away. "I'll try to be there."

"You have to be there, bro. Operation Get Mom off the Ground and Across the Ocean begins that night."

"If I can get away, I'll be there. And maybe with a date."

Jason whistled. "It's Skylar, isn't it? I know you've

had a thing for her for a long time. Good for you, bro. She's a smart one."

"She is. Thanks again, Jason. If I see you this weekend, I see you. I can't make any promises."

"I understand. You've got an important case."

"Do you really understand?"

"I do. I know I razz you a lot. And I'm sorry. But you are the twerp of the family. Just comes with the territory. Talk to you later."

His brother hung up, and Joe picked up the notes he'd scribbled while talking: "Truckers transporting black market eagle parts across the US."

Most likely using the Indian reservations as contact points.

"Malcolm Davis is picking up customers at powwows," Joe muttered. "Has to be."

Now he remembered the freezers Skylar had mentioned seeing in the warehouse. Surely a trucking outfit stored product and had surplus. And yet, it wouldn't make good financial sense to store things. They transported goods from one location to the other. If they had something stored in those freezers, it had to be something that required being kept on ice.

Joe clicked the mouse and searched the database for shipping records connected to local businesses and the Duluth port. He needed to track all the pickups made by Davis Trucking.

And then determine how close they were to the local Indian reservations.

Chapter Twenty-One

Skylar set the chicken feed in the back of her truck. The farm-supply store carried everything from feed to tires to even some clothing and candy.

At the sound of a car horn, she turned. Joe Cash waved at her from his truck. Instantly her body warmed with a hot, liquid sensation from having lain next to him all night. That man knew how to kiss. And use his mouth on all the right places on her body. She waved and stepped around the side of the truck to lean against the back of it as he pulled into the empty parking lot and got out.

He hooked his hands in his front pockets and tilted his head. "Miss me?"

Skylar started to laugh, but then decided it wasn't funny. Hell, yes, she'd missed him standing close to her, close enough to smell his wild woods scent and to feel her skin tingle at memory of their lovemaking.

"Am I supposed to?" she asked with as much indifference as she could muster.

"Is that how it's going to work?" Joe rubbed his jaw and cast a glance down the main street. The Dairy

Queen sported a queue of teenagers outside the walk-up window.

"No, it's not. I'd hug you, but…" Now Skylar glanced around.

"You don't want anyone to see? Wow." Joe dropped his shoulders and whistled lowly. "You ashamed of being seen with me, Skylar?"

"No. I just—I don't know what's going on between us. I'd love to grab you right now and pull you in for a kiss, but is that real? I mean, was last night just a hookup?"

"I already told you how I feel about it." The man had a sweet way of looking down, which almost made him look shy. "Ball's in your court now."

Was she sure of what she'd thought it had been? It had been more than a night of sex. Right? Was it too soon to get involved with another man? Ending it with Cole had put her through the emotional wringer. And now with everything else…

"I'm sorry," Joe offered. "This thing between us is probably weird. There's an active investigation going on, and you're involved. I don't want to blur any lines between investigating officer and victim."

"I don't like being called a victim."

"You're not. You were a target. And so was Stella. But I like you, Skylar. Always have. Always will. And I'm not a one-night-stand kind of guy. But I don't want to freak you out, either. You might very well have thought it was just a one-time thing."

"I didn't, but I'm not sure…"

"You don't have to make any major life decisions right now. I'm ready whenever you are."

She nodded. "So you'll let me take a step back and figure out what I want and what I need?"

"I'm good with that."

"No, you're not." His body language screamed for her to embrace him. And hers was screaming much the same, though she held her arms over her chest to stop from flinging herself into those muscled arms.

He shrugged. "Have to be. I don't want to hurt you, Skylar. Not like—" The man blew out a heavy breath and ran his fingers through that thick dark hair she could still feel brushing her skin.

"What is it?" She stepped up to him and studied his elusive gaze. When he finally did meet her eyes, his wince did not bode well. "Joe?"

"Ah, it's Cole Pruitt."

"We're not together anymore. I promise you that. I don't know how much more of a message I can send than a burned wedding dress."

"It's not that. I know the two of you are through. That comes across loud and clear to me. It's just, the interrogation this morning."

"Did you get what you needed from him? He wasn't the one who shot at me, was he?"

"I don't think so. Though I do suspect he's doing something underhanded for Malcolm. But he's not talking. And he insists he won't talk to anyone but you. Which is ridiculous. You're not the one investigating this case. And as far as I'm concerned, I intend to keep that man as far away from you—"

She gripped his shirt. "I'll talk to him."

"What? No, Skylar. He's doing this to manipulate. I can't let him have the upper hand."

"He's a stubborn asshole."

"He was never like that when I was friends with him. I think the drinking has changed him."

"I think so, too. I don't want to see him again, but if he'll tell me what's going on, I can do that for you."

"I don't want you to have to do anything for me, Skylar."

"Then how are you going to make him talk? Don't you want to solve this case? Protect me? What about Max Owen? Don't you want answers about him?"

"Max is first and foremost in my mind. But he's gone. There's nothing I can do to bring him back."

"Who was he to you, Joe? He must have been very special…"

He bowed his head and winced.

"If you don't want to tell me, I won't push."

Joe flipped his hair from his brow with a brush of his hand. The way the sunlight caught in his eyes shouldn't be so deliciously tantalizing.

When he turned back to her, he bowed his head and spoke quietly, as if imparting a secret. "Remember when I told you about getting lost in the woods for three days?"

"Of course. I even looked it up online. You were led out by wolves. That was amazing."

"Yeah, but there's a part I never told anyone about. I didn't want him to get in trouble."

"Him?"

"Max Owen camped in the woods every summer. He's the one who found me wandering, lost and hungry. He fed me and cared for me those three days. Taught me things."

Skylar narrowed her gaze on Joe. This didn't sound good.

"It's not like that," he quickly added. "He didn't do anything to me. He was a kind old Native American man who answered all the questions an eager ten-year-old boy had about how the wolves can understand one another when they howl. And why the moss only grows on one side of the trees. And how to make my own tepee. I wasn't scared, and I honestly didn't want to go home. In those few days Max taught me a lot. But he was the one who said I needed to go home. That my parents would be worried."

"I recall they organized a search party."

"Yes, but they didn't get far. Max sent me home with the wolves."

Skylar didn't know what to say to that. It was beautiful. And that experience must have been what set Joe on his path to work as a conservation officer.

"Max had an affinity for a pack that lived close to him. It was the same pack that had tracked me as I'd wandered deeper into the woods and gotten lost. I was never once scared or worried they might attack me. Weird, huh? If I'd known better at the time, I would have been freaked."

"Wolves do track humans, and if they are frail or the wolves are hungry..." Skylar hadn't heard of any humans being attacked by wolves lately, though on occasion, some stupid hiker who tried to approach the wild animal could get bitten. And a frightened, ten-year-old child alone in the woods could look like an easy meal to a pack.

"Max said they were keeping an eye on me. Protecting me. And they did lead me home. I started researching wolves and wildlife the moment I got home. Well, after Mom made me shower and made me my favorite macaroni and cheese. Guess I've been a nature boy ever since."

"And Max?" Skylar prompted. "You hadn't seen him since you were ten?"

"No, I uh…visited a lot after that. I'd tell my parents I was going on a scouting trip or staying with a friend, and then make my way to where Max stayed. It was about half a day's hike from the entrance to the Boundary Waters Canoe Wilderness. And two miles from where they found Max lying roadside, dying. He was poisoned, Skylar." He looked across the street, the sun again glinting in his eyes.

Skylar swallowed and nudged her shoulder against his. "I'm so sorry, Joe. I had no idea what the old man meant to you. Thank you for telling me that."

"I've never told anyone about Max. Didn't want him to get arrested or to lead the media closer to him. He didn't own the plot where he camped, but I'd be damned if I was going to turn him in for squatting."

"No, you protected him. Just as you're protecting me now. And I appreciate that, Joe, but you need to step back and allow me to help you. For Max."

She crossed her arms and waited for the man to accept her offer. Cole was personable and a charmer, and, yes, she'd fallen for him because of those attributes. But she'd quickly learned just how deep his stubborn streak ran. If the man wanted something—like to talk to her—then he could hold out for days, weeks even, until he got his way.

"Is there some kind of room where you can observe while I talk to the guy?" she asked. "Like on TV?"

"The interrogation room. Yes. But Skylar…"

"You know there's no other way. Cole will keep his mouth shut if he thinks that'll piss you off. And I'll be across the table from him, right? He won't be able to touch me?"

"He'd be in cuffs and chained to the table or floor. I still haven't agreed to allow you to do this."

"I'm offering my services as a citizen, Joe. It would be a pity if you didn't take advantage of my kindness, and if I had to go over your head to whoever is your superior…"

"You wouldn't do that."

"I can and I will. I want the poaching to stop as much as you do. And if I can help, I will."

Joe heaved out a breath. He rubbed his pinky finger along the side of her hand and hooked it with hers. Finally she slid her hand into his and squeezed, and she let him pull her into a hug. Right there, standing in the empty parking lot, which was clearly visible to all who drove by on Main Street. She didn't care because, right now, the only place she wanted to be was in Joe's arms.

"I'm charging him with drunk driving and reckless

endangerment. But I'm sure, much as he denies it, he went after you with purpose."

"I hate to consider it, but you may be right."

He hugged her tighter. "I don't want him breathing the same air as you, but if this is what it takes…"

"I'll be fine as long as I know you're close."

"I'll be on the other side of the door. Promise."

"Okay." She tilted up on her toes and kissed him. But only a quick kiss. Much as her body had already decided it was all in for Joe Cash, her heart was still leery. And feeding the gossip mill was not what she needed right now. "Let's go there now."

"I have to coordinate with a fellow officer from the sheriff's department and verify some military records. Might take some time. How about you cruise over to the DQ and get yourself a treat, then I'll see you at the station in an hour?"

"I can do that."

She started to pull away, but Joe's clasp on her hand held firm. He lifted her hand and kissed it. "I wish it could have been different," he said. "I wish you'd never gotten involved with Cole."

Some days she wished for the same. "A person makes choices, whether good, bad or ugly, and learns from those choices. That's the way the world works, Joe. I don't dwell on mistakes, because some are meant for teaching."

He heaved out a sigh, and she disengaged from their clasped hands. "Think about it. You'll understand. I'll see you in a bit."

He watched her pull out of the parking lot and over

to the main road. Yeah, she'd made a mistake with Cole. But she had learned a lesson. Follow her head and let her stupid heart take a pass. And now she was moving forward.

Next step? Figuring out what sort of pace she could manage.

Chapter Twenty-Two

Allowing Skylar to sit in the interrogation room alone with Cole Pruitt was trying every ounce of Joe's restraint. He'd cuffed Pruitt behind the back and through the chair so he couldn't move forward to try to touch Skylar. But he'd caught Cole's wink toward the two-way glass as he'd watched Skylar take a seat across the table from him.

The man was purposely trying to piss him off. And while he thought he could manipulate him by talking to Skylar, Joe was not going to take the bait. He could remain calm and listen without anger while the two talked.

Skylar took off her cowboy hat and set it on the table while Cole smirked at her. She glanced over her shoulder to the glass, which would not reveal Joe's position to them. Still, she gave him a small smile.

He wanted to rush in there and pull her out. To not allow Cole one more moment breathing the same air as her. He didn't deserve that time alone with her.

Joe turned to the clerk sitting before the recording console. "You recording?"

"Yes, sir."

He'd told Skylar to try to stick to the points: who Cole was working for and what, exactly, he was involved in. He'd warned her Cole would try to talk about anything other than those topics. He hadn't brought up his suspicions about the sniper. He could ask about that himself. She could handle this. He knew that she could.

"Long time no see," Cole drawled.

"Not exactly," Skylar said. She tucked her fingers under each thigh and sat straight on the chair, her back to Joe. "You waved to me in the Supply Mart parking lot last month as I was driving out."

"And you didn't wave back."

"I'm not here to reminisce, or to seek some sort of coming to terms between the two of us. We're over, and you know that. Joe needs answers from you, and apparently you're only willing to give those answers to me. So talk."

"You've become harsh, Skylar. You weren't like this when we started dating."

"Our dating history has no relevance to this conversation."

She was doing well, but still Joe winced. It could only get worse for her. And his heart.

"You lied to Joe," Skylar said. "You told him it was you who left me at the altar."

Cole shrugged. "You left me. I left you. Doesn't matter, does it? As you've said, it's over. For both of us."

"That it is. I could never remain in the life of someone involved in poaching. And what's this about the

DUI? You never drank so much. It's beneath you, Cole. You're a better man than that."

Cole tilted his head and eyed the glass, as if he could see through to Joe. "Is Joe your better man?"

"I don't understand," Skylar said.

"I always wondered if it was him you wanted instead of me. Whenever his name would come up in conversation you'd get a big smile on your face. Guess I know the answer to that now. You've hooked up with him mighty fast."

"It's none of your business who I decide to have in my life."

Cole leaned forward. "Have you had sex with him?"

Joe gripped his fists tight. The clerk at his side shifted on his chair. He didn't want anyone else to hear this. Cole had become mean. It had to be the booze. Had working for Davis pushed him to drink?

"My sex life is also none of your business," Skylar said. She lifted her head. "Answers are what I came for. Who are you working for, Cole? It's Malcolm, isn't it?"

"You have," he said, ignoring her questions. "I can smell him on you."

Joe paced toward the door but stopped himself from gripping the handle. Just give her a moment, he told himself. She was so close.

"Tell me you loved me," Cole suddenly said.

Skylar leaned back in her chair.

"You did, didn't you?" Cole challenged.

She lifted her chin, unwilling to give him an answer.

"You don't give me answers, I don't give you answers."

"What do you want to hear?" she asked.

"The truth. You give me your truth, I'll give you mine." Again Cole cast a glance toward the glass, seeming to pinpoint Joe with precision.

"The truth?" Skylar blew out a breath.

Joe watched her shoulders slump. He didn't want to hear this. He should rush in there now and put a stop to this.

"I'm not even sure I know what love is, Cole. I thought I loved you. Maybe I did. More likely, it was some kind of lust. I was trying to fill a need, but it wasn't a real, honest need. Do *you* know what love is?"

The man straightened at the abrupt spin on the question. "Well, I don't know. I know you were the prettiest girl I'd ever met, and I was ready to make a life with you."

"Sure, but I heard no mention of love in that statement."

He sighed and bowed his head.

Joe's attention grew fierce.

"Fine," Cole said. "As long as Cash can promise me there won't be any charges other than the DUI, I'll give him names."

Joe tapped the intercom and said, "As soon as bail is posted, you'll be released for the DUI until a summons is set, then the judge will likely revoke your license for a year. You'll be driving with whiskey plates for a year after that. No other charges. Promise."

Cole sneered. "Whiskey plates. Remember how we used to joke about those poor fellas who had to drive around with those flags on the tail end of their trucks, Joe?"

"It's a hell of a lot better than attempted murder," Skylar said bluntly.

"I didn't want to hurt you, Skylar. I was drunk. Angry. I…"

"Did you poison Stella?"

Cole looked up. "What? No. I would never. I loved that wolf. I mean, I tolerated her. But I would never harm an animal—" Cole tilted back his head and then surrendered. "Fine. I should have never gotten involved with that slimy bastard in the first place. You promise me some protection, Joe?"

Joe pressed the intercom. "If it's warranted, yes."

Cole nodded. "So I've been poaching for Malcolm. The old man's got me for a loan on my boat and I need to pay him off. But I won't be driving any trucks for him again."

Joe tapped the intercom once more. "Why would you be driving trucks?"

Cole squeezed his eyelids shut for a few moments. "They're running parts throughout the states and I believe they have a few routes going to the southern border of the United States. I almost got stopped at the Canadian border last week. I hate that subterfuge crap. I just want to fish and—hell, have a normal life."

Joe leaned forward and pressed the intercom again. "What parts?"

"Ah, hell. Bear organs. Deer antlers. Eagle talons, feathers and beaks. Davis goes to the powwows and finds buyers. He just lost a tribe in the area and was pissed about it. Some old man talked the tribe into waiting for the confiscated evidence the sheriff releases. That's all I know."

Joe tapped the button again. "Thanks, Cole. I'm going to come in and verify those statements, and we'll let Skylar take a break, okay?"

The man nodded, then bowed his head until his forehead rested on the table.

SKYLAR DECIDED NOT to wait for Joe to come out of the station. He could be a while longer with Cole. And much as she wanted to walk back into his arms and resume their hug, she suspected Joe might be a little twitchy about her after talking to Cole. She'd give him some space this afternoon. But she did plan on inviting him over for supper, so she drove to the grocery store.

Gathering lettuce, walnuts, dried cranberries and an interesting raspberry vinaigrette, she then picked up a bottle of wine.

"Wining and dining," she muttered as she walked out to the truck and put the grocery bags in the passenger side.

She stepped back and felt arms go around her waist. A hand clamped across her mouth. Kicking and struggling, Skylar was able to see only that no one was nearby in the parking lot to witness what was happening to her. Whoever had her carried her around the side of the grocery store and stuffed a cloth in her mouth before she could utter a scream. Her hands were wrenched behind her back and cuffed.

Lifted none too gently, she was tossed into the back of a black SUV that did not have license plates. Rolling onto her side, she only saw the torsos of a large man and another wearing an AC/DC T-shirt before the back hatch was shut. The windows were blackened, so she couldn't make out their faces.

The front and passenger doors slammed shut, and the vehicle took off. No one spoke. Skylar cursed her decision not to wait for Joe by the police station.

Chapter Twenty-Three

Cole signed the statement verifying his confession. He'd spend another few days in county jail, unless his bail was met. If the investigation was still active at that time, Joe would assess the man's need for police protection. And then the county judge would hear Cole's plea in a few weeks. Joe had given him the contact info for the local AA meetings. He hoped the man had the courage to go to one. But if he didn't get out from under Malcolm Davis's thumb, that would never happen.

With Cole's statement that Reginald Marshall was a sharpshooter, and owned some black market rifles, Joe could now get a warrant to search the man's property. Cole didn't know about his military history, but he said Reggie, as they called him, was Malcolm's right-hand man. Unfortunately, the judge was taking his time, said he needed to do some research. At the very least, Joe had a few hours to waste before he might hold the warrant in hand. He was suspicious of the judge's delay. The man was generally punctual. He certainly hoped he wasn't one of the men Malcolm had in his pocket.

He'd missed Skylar after the interrogation, so he

planned to drive out to her place to thank her and to see how she was holding up. Cole had been malicious, but she had held her own. That didn't mean she hadn't been hurt by the experience, however.

First he stopped at home for a quick bite to eat. Joe locked the truck and wandered up the short sidewalk to his front stoop. There on the top step lay something under a sheet of newspaper. Joe's hackles immediately went up. He cast a glance around the yard, across the street and over the neighborhood. He took in all the house fronts, the shrubs, searching for anyone watching from behind a curtain or tree cover. The sun was setting, shadowing the opposite side of the street before the houses. But he didn't feel as though he was being watched.

Cautiously, Joe knelt and nudged aside the paper with the toe of his shoe. The bottom portion of an eagle body was revealed, talons curled under. Joe sucked in his breath. He immediately pulled out a pair of latex gloves from inside his jacket and tugged them on.

Carefully removing the paper, he then folded it and tucked it under the eagle's body. He didn't want to discard any evidence. The bird's wings were tucked in, as well as its head. It may have once been frozen, for it was still rigid; the head didn't joggle when he touched it. Yet it didn't feel cold. He didn't want to touch it too much, so he walked back to the truck to grab an evidence bag.

Again his eyes took in the neighborhood. Sunlight beamed low on his house, giving the lower portion that golden-hour glow. Someone may have seen who had been on his property. On the other hand, he hadn't been home since this morning. This could have been here all day.

Though he'd expect some insect activity if that was the case.

As he walked back to the step, he glanced toward the corner of the house and just under the soffit. The small green LED confirmed his security camera was still on. He'd know soon enough who had been on his property.

After bagging the eagle, he called the forensic lab van. They weren't anywhere near town, but would drive through in the morning. He'd have to wait until then to turn over the evidence.

Carrying it inside, he thought about placing it in the freezer, but if any poison was on it, that could contaminate the entire kitchen. Instead he set it out in an empty box in the garage. Then he peeled off the gloves and placed them in the box, as well. His next step was to shed his clothing and place that in a separate garbage bag. Forensics might want to test them, and he certainly didn't want them anywhere near his home.

Wondering who had decided he needed to be threatened, Joe stalked down the hallway to the bathroom to take a long shower.

JOE KNOCKED ON Skylar's door and waited. Within ten seconds of the knock, he sensed the curious wolf peeking around the corner of the cabin.

"Hey, Stella!"

The wolf wandered toward him, head down and eyes up. She held her tail low, as if she was afraid or perhaps cautious.

"What's up, sweetie?" Joe squatted, putting himself at her height. He held out his hand, which she sniffed, then nudged once with her muzzle. Stella then loped down the steps to the ground and waited for him. Still no tail wag.

"You want to play fetch or something? I need to see your person first. Make sure everything is cool with her." He glanced over his shoulder. "Is she home? It's been a couple hours since I spoke to her in town."

Stella yipped and walked toward the corner of the house. *Follow me.*

Joe stepped down and followed the wolf's slow steps. Perhaps Skylar was out back doing something and hadn't heard the doorbell. He rounded the side of the house to the backyard. A quick scan showed no sign of the sexy blonde with the slender curves and ever-present cowboy hat. Becky raced out of sight, but Joe just caught a flash of her new red sweater. Beyoncé was nowhere to be seen, thank goodness. He wondered if his vehicle insurance covered dents inflicted by a dancing goat.

His cell phone jangled in his front pocket, but Joe ignored it as he searched the glimmering lake beyond the tree line. The sun had almost set, yet dashed a tinsel of light across the water.

Stella yipped. Right at his side.

"What is it, Stella?"

The phone was still ringing so Joe answered it. "Officer Cash."

"Joe, just listen and let me talk."

It was Skylar and she sounded…not right. Opening

his mouth to respond, he instead nodded, and then re-membered she couldn't see him. "Go ahead."

"I'm okay," she said.

Those two abrupt words put up the hairs on the back of his neck. No one started a conversation with "I'm okay" unless they were not, or darn close to not.

"I'm with…people."

He heard a shuffle and Skylar's gasp. Had she been shoved?

"The Davises," she amended.

"What? Skylar—"

"No time for conversation, Joe. They picked me up outside the grocery store. They know Cole told you ev-erything, and they're going to let me go free—"

"Go free?" Hell, Malcolm Davis had kidnapped Sky-lar? Joe gripped the gun handle in its holster.

"You have to drop all charges against Cole Pruitt and drop the investigation," Skylar continued. "Please, Joe. I've never asked you for anything. I need this."

"Where are they holding you?"

"Not sure."

"At Davis Trucking?"

"Don't think so. It's dark in here."

"How are you talking—? Oh, they've got you on speaker. You bastards. You think leaving a poisoned eagle on my doorstep is going to scare me off, Davis?"

"Joe, please, they're going to hang up. As soon as the investigation is dropped and they know you won't bother them again—ever—they'll let me go."

"How the hell will I prove that?"

"I've been told to tell you they will know if you stop investigating."

Right. Because Joe's suspicion about Malcolm having the judge in his pocket was true. Could be the reason he was currently waiting for the warrant.

"Will you do me a favor?" Skylar made a painful noise.

Joe winced. They were hurting her.

"Check on Stella!" she quickly cried. "Talk to her!"

The phone clicked off. Joe punched the air with his phone, then kicked the ground with his heel. He swore. Once, then again. The blood rushed to his face and arms. Fists curled. He had to find Skylar. And he would not drop the investigation. He'd spent far too much time investigating the poaching, and with the poisoned eagle left on his doorstep he now had a link to Max Owen's death. Malcolm Davis knew his number was up.

So he'd kidnapped an innocent woman—his own niece—to hold up as his shield. The coward.

Joe swore again. He had to take a moment to think this through, plan his next move. He couldn't rush in, guns blazing, because Skylar didn't know where she was being held. It made sense that it was on Davis Trucking property.

Stalking back to his truck, he called up Dispatch.

They answered immediately. "I've got a situation at Davis Trucking," Joe said. "At least, it's a suspicion."

"Aren't you waiting on a warrant for that place?"

"I am. But I have reason to believe Skylar Davis is being held against her will there right now. I'm headed there."

When he turned, Stella sat waiting for him. She tilted

her head, one ear cocked. Her whimper indicated she felt for him.

What had Skylar meant about *talking to Stella*? At a moment when she could be in danger and possibly be harmed, she had wanted him to talk to her wolf?

"I'll send out Brent Kofax," Dispatch said. "He's finishing up a domestic call right now. Shouldn't be too long."

"Thanks. I'm on my way there." He hung up and then ruffled Stella's fur behind her ears. "She loves you," he said to the wolf.

Stella scampered across the backyard toward the edge of the forest. She stopped and looked back at Joe. Never had an animal's expression spoken more loudly than it did in Stella's quiet gold eyes.

"You do want to tell me something, don't you?" he said.

The wolf was smart as hell. And Skylar's best friend. If Skylar wanted him to talk to Stella, then he would.

THE BLINDFOLD SMELLED like oil. And Skylar couldn't get a handle on where she was being held. They had traveled about half an hour after she'd been taken and thrown into the back of the SUV. She knew there were two men, and both had guns. Malcolm wasn't around. Or was he? He could be standing by, watching. In fact, she had the creepy feeling the men were being directed.

Was she at Davis Trucking? No way to know for sure, and she hadn't wanted to send Joe on a wrong path if it were not.

"I know you're here, Malcolm," she said. And to

challenge him, she added, "And I know you had Max Owen killed."

A chair scraped on the cement floor. Someone gripped Skylar's hair and pulled back her head. The blindfold was roughly tugged away. Whoever held her from behind pushed her head forward.

Skylar gasped when she saw who stood before her.

Chapter Twenty-Four

The wolf tracked steadily through the woods from Skylar's place. Joe kept up with Stella, even when she veered from a path and wandered into brush and low seedlings and mossy ground. It was Stella's show, and he was thankful she seemed intent and focused on getting somewhere.

Where was she headed? Joe hoped she was leading him to Skylar, but they could be headed anywhere. The pack's abandoned rendezvous spot sat parallel to where they now passed. He could smell the lake and the cloying scents of animal.

He pulled out his cell phone. No service. With luck, Kofax's domestic call wouldn't keep him long, and he'd be on his way to Davis Trucking. Joe wore a pistol in his hip holster, and always carried a bowie knife that was useful for hacking through saplings and whittling off kindling from larger branches. It could be used for defense in a pinch. But he had no flashlight on him, and should have grabbed one out of his truck before leaving on this expedition.

Didn't matter. He felt more confident in the dark

woods than a man might walking down a sunlit street in a dangerous part of Duluth. But he did need to be cautious for traps. Unfortunately, if they happened upon one, Stella would be the first to step into it, and that wolf could not spare another leg.

The *po-po-po* whistle of a boreal owl made Stella pause. Joe stopped roughly twenty feet behind the wolf's tread. Stella whined lowly and sniffed the ground. She cautiously stepped on the loamy earth, covered with rotting leaves and branches, and then leaped back and walked a half circle, drawing her once-straight path into an arc.

She looked to Joe, waiting for him to do the same. He did. And when he passed the brush where the wolf had spooked, he smelled the spoiled bait that sat on a steel trap.

"Thanks, Stella," he said quietly. "I imagine you've got a sixth sense about traps now, eh?" It was on Skylar's property. Damn Malcolm Davis. "Are you taking me to Skylar?"

The wolf turned and wandered forward, nose to the ground and tail bobbing side to side. Not talkative, but then it wasn't necessary.

After they'd tracked for what Joe estimated to be about two miles, they reached a clearing where the tree canopy opened to frame the waxing moon. As Stella kept walking, Joe cast his gaze upward and studied the stars. The Big Dipper was in view, and Arcturus beamed brightly. They were moving northwest of the property. If he recalled correctly the map he'd looked over, that meant they were either currently on DNR-owned property, passing over that small thumb of it, or already on someone else's land.

"Malcolm's land," he muttered.

He hadn't noticed any trespassing signs, and for sure that family would post. Then again, he wasn't on a trail.

Branches snapped, and he steadied his footsteps to land more lightly on the ground. He didn't want to alert anyone out patrolling or trip any security systems. There could be motion sensors. Hell, there could be booby traps, for all he knew. The family that poached would not risk intruders getting too close to their property.

Of course, they would not be prepared for a wolf's wily approach, or the man who could move like a wolf.

The scent of burning peat filtered into Joe's senses. A bonfire close by? He didn't see the flames, though the woods had thickened and Stella's steps had slowed. When he got closer to her, he crouched. The wolf turned to nudge his face with her head. A sign of affection, perhaps even trust.

"Is this where you wanted to lead me, sweetie?"

She pawed at the brush, and Joe realized it was matted up against a fence post. Higher up, strung around the post, a single wire was wrapped. Electrified, if his guess was correct. He tugged out the knife from his pocket. It had a wood handle, so if the fence was turned on, the handle would prevent the charge from shocking his hand. Rubbing quickly over the wire, Joe felt the tingle of current.

"Thanks for the warning, Stella. Let's take it easy from here on."

Because now they were encroaching on private property. Joe tugged out his phone again. One bar. He could make a call. He needed that warrant if this was a false lead and Skylar was being kept elsewhere.

When the sound of a rifle shot echoed through the night, he held the glowing phone close to his chest and ducked down next to the wolf, who stood rigid, and growled low and deep in her chest.

SKYLAR SAT STIFFLY on the chair. Her wrists burned from the rough rope they'd used to tie her, but the rope at her left ankle was loosening. She shifted her boot heel back and forth, firmly tugging while keeping an eye on the guy with the semiautomatic who stood guard beside her. The same redhead who had threatened her days earlier.

But he gave her much less worry than the other person who stood before her—a woman she hadn't seen in seventeen years.

Her mother looked the same, save the weary lines under her eyes and around her mouth. Her blond hair was styled in a flipped bob, and the bright pink lipstick was still the same shade Skylar remembered.

Her heart raced. Every part of her wanted to scream and then cry and then shout her anger.

"I had to leave," her mother said dismissively. "I wasn't happy with my life, but that was my problem. Not yours. I wanted to contact you. But I thought it wiser to stay away. Let you and your dad have your peace. I've been catching up with old friends this past week."

Old friends? Meaning Skylar's uncle? Dorothy's brother-in-law?

Dorothy leaned forward and pouted her pink lips. "You should let Malcolm help you with the shelter."

"Help me? I'm tied up, Dorothy." It felt strange to say that name after so long. But she couldn't summon the word "mom." It felt dirty in her throat.

"The ties are just a precaution. And since when did you stop calling me Mom?"

"When you abandoned me and Dad."

"That was long ago, Skylar. We're both grown and wiser now. So just shush, and play along, okay? Malcolm needs to get the game warden off his back. He's not like the others."

"The others?" It was no secret her uncle had a cop or two in his pocket. Was he trying to recruit Joe to do his dirty work?

"No one will get hurt."

"Someone has been murdered, Dorothy."

Malcolm walked over to join them, hands in his pockets and cowboy boots clicking the concrete floor. "What's that about murder? You telling your mother lies, Skylar?"

When the rifle sounded outside the shed, all the men inside volleyed looks at one another. Skylar's guard moved closer to her and lifted his gun into position.

"What's up?" Malcolm asked the guard named Reggie. "You got the guard dog out there?"

"He croaked last week. I sent Steven out on post. Must have heard something or got spooked."

"Maybe it's Cash," Malcolm said.

"He's not stupid enough to come looking for me in

the dark with a warehouse full of armed men waiting for him," Skylar said.

Malcolm rounded a look on her. "He isn't? Or is he? I figured you'd be the invite he required. Unless he's suddenly fallen ill."

Reggie smirked. "I hear that cop is a nature boy. Really likes his animals. He'd be real sad to see a dead eagle on his doorstep. Might hold it a bit too long."

"What's this about an eagle on Cash's doorstep?" Cole Pruitt crossed the warehouse, hands in his pockets. He didn't even glance at Skylar.

She hadn't realized he was in the building. How was he out of jail? Joe had said he'd be in— There were too many emotions wrenching at her heart right now; she couldn't think straight.

"None of your damn business, Cole," Malcolm said. "Go out and check on Steven."

"I'm not leaving this warehouse." Cole crossed his arms stubbornly, high over his chest.

"You are the only one available. And I did post your bail. Now go take a look!"

Skylar had never seen Cole so submissive. Head hanging, he turned and stalked toward the double barn doors at the end of the warehouse. That left her, Reggie and one other man, who also wielded a rifle, by the door. And her mother. Dorothy. Back from a seventeen-year absence, acting as if it had been a day. Telling Skylar to play along?

Had Dorothy ever loved her father? In those weeks before her mother had left them, Skylar had overheard her parents arguing. Malcolm's name had come up a lot. Her twelve-year-old self hadn't put two and two together. But years later, Skylar had wondered if her mother had a thing for the other brother. So why not simply divorce the one and take up with the other? Why abandon her family?

And now here she stood, siding with the one man who had tried his best over the years to make his brother's life hell. And had he done so by being the one who had prompted his wife to leave him?

Skylar expected nothing more from Malcolm. Or Dorothy.

By using her to call Joe and request he drop the investigation, Malcolm had known what he was doing. How he knew she and Joe had a relationship was beyond her.

They never should have kissed in that parking lot. Someone must have seen them.

On the other hand, Cole could have told him things. He'd picked up on her feelings for Joe when she'd spoken to him in the interrogation room. She should have never agreed to talk to him.

And why she was muddling over this stuff right now, when she needed to remain alert, was beyond her. She'd heard the howls earlier. Pack howls. Miles off, but in the direction of her land. They'd been disturbed, had seen something.

She just hoped the pack hadn't decided to stop that something.

Chapter Twenty-Five

Joe sat crouched in the brush, sure he was hidden from the dark figure who stalked along the birch tree line that paralleled a massive Quonset shed. This must be the back end of Davis Trucking. The shed was small compared to the vinyl-sided building next to it. That building must house the trucks and perhaps serve as a shop for the scents of oil and gasoline that filled the air.

A flicker of fire showed between the two buildings. Joe couldn't see anyone standing near the bonfire tending it, but it was a good three hundred yards off and the darkness hugged the amber flames.

He rested his hand at the back of Stella's neck, urging her to be silent, but the wolf was smart. She remained alert, her head lifted and sniffing the air.

Suddenly, he felt her entire body tense and she shifted to her feet.

Joe heard someone call out. "What the hell, Steven? You shooting at ghosts?"

It was Cole Pruitt. Stella recognized his scent.

Joe shushed her low growl and stroked down her

neck. She kept on her feet and shifted, but didn't vo-
calize further, thank goodness.

How had Pruitt gotten out of jail? Had someone paid
his bail? Likely Malcolm Davis. Damn it, what had Cole
gotten himself into? Had he taken Skylar?

"Thought I should fire off a warning shot," said the
other man, who had been pacing alongside the birch
trees. "Just in case. You think it was stupid for the old
man to have the woman call a cop?"

"Maybe. But Malcolm generally knows what he's
doing."

Joe watched the shadowed figures. They stood fifty
feet from him and Stella, backs to them. Moonlight
capped their heads and gleamed on Cole's nose when
he turned to face the other man. "Not like the old man
doesn't have half the cops in the county in his pocket.
Probably time to bring another one in, don't you think?"

"I think it's stupid." The other guy spit on the ground.

Stella sat, still alert, listening. Joe rested his shoulder
against her body. It reassured him of her movements
and kept him close enough to grab for her in case she
decided to take off, but he did not expect that from this
wolf. She was too damn smart.

"We should just kill that woman and get on with
things."

"You're talking about my ex-fiancée," Cole said.

"She must be ex for a reason. Don't you want to stick
it to the woman who dumped you?"

"I dumped her," Cole said quickly. "And you don't
get to talk about the Davis woman that way. She's not
to be harmed."

"She'll talk."

"She won't. And that other woman is her mother. She'll make sure Skylar keeps her mouth shut."

"Is that so?"

Joe winced. Skylar's mom was here? But she had left her family long ago. What was going on?

"You check all the borders behind the building?" Cole asked.

"Was going to head around to the other side and take a piss."

"Didn't need to know about that. I'll let the old man know everything is clear."

"Don't worry, I got my eyes peeled. Nothing will get past me and this thirty-aught-six."

"I am completely reassured," Cole said.

Joe knew from his tone that he was anything but. The men parted, Cole heading toward the building and the other veering around the back of it.

Joe could wait for Kofax to arrive, but he had no idea how long that would take. And he couldn't stand knowing that Skylar was inside that building in God-knows-what condition with the asshole Cole Pruitt standing over her.

Pulling out his gun, he allowed Stella to sniff it. She whined lowly, but the sound was so soft he knew the man tromping around the back of the shed would not hear.

"You need to stay here, sweetie."

For as much as he was comfortable with wolves and could communicate his emotions and understand theirs, Joe knew she couldn't comprehend such a request. For her safety, he hoped she would remain hidden. The first thing a poacher would do on sighting a wolf was shoot. They had no conscience and always preferred a dead wolf to a live one that could attack.

Not that he suspected Stella had it in her to attack. She was a softy. And he wanted to keep her that way.

Rising slowing to a crouch, he said, "Stay," even though he figured Skylar hadn't taught her any commands.

The wolf sat and looked up at him, giving him that innocent, wondering gaze that most dogs had mastered and that could bring their owner to their knees for a hug and a tussle.

"I'm going to get your person," Joe said. "You keep watch for me out here. Don't make a noise." He shushed the wolf, then started toward the line of birch trees.

To her credit, Stella remained where she was sitting.

When he reached the edge of the white paper birch trees, Joe pressed his shoulder to one and scanned around the building. The lighting was dim, but there was a spotlight on the left side where he guessed the main doors were. The bonfire was too far off to provide illumination of more than a few feet. The guard had been around the other side for about three minutes. If he were pissing, he'd be done by now. But would he stay on that side? Joe wouldn't.

He had to move now.

Stepping lightly, he raced across the dirt and grass to the side of the building. Once tucked into the shadows, he hugged the corrugated metal wall and slinked toward the corner.

He heard a scuffle at the other end of the building. It was the guard. Joe pressed his back to the ridged wall, feeling the darkness cover him and knowing he was concealed, but essentially standing in the open, without protection.

The guard wandered to the birch trees. He moved his gaze upward. Stars littered the sky, and the moonlight would give him away if Joe moved so much as three inches forward. He waited for the stargazer to lose interest, but he kept his head tilted back for the longest time.

Joe began to inch to the right. The corner of the building was ten feet away. If he could get around to the other side—and into the spotlight—

Hell, was he crazy?

He should wait for backup. But by then it could be too late. What were they doing with Skylar in there? If they'd had her call him and stop the investigation, there was no need to keep her prisoner. He should have told them he'd agree. But would they really have released her? He didn't suspect so. The only way Skylar was walking away from Malcolm's grip alive was with help.

And her mother. Was she a hostage or an accomplice?

The guard suddenly glanced toward the woods. Had Stella alerted him?

If he wondered about the wolf's safety he could lose his own chance for movement, so Joe stepped faster until his shoulder felt nothing. He'd reached the corner.

He sensed the guard turn toward him, so Joe slipped around the side of the building and out of his sight. Taking in the area, he saw no one standing outside. There were three vehicles parked before the shed. That could mean anywhere from three men up to a dozen or more were inside, depending on how many they'd stuffed into each vehicle. Two buildings down, a diesel engine fired up. A truck heading out on a night route? Sure, truck drivers drove all hours of the day, but the timing was suspicious.

Joe needed backup to hurry.

Raising his pistol and gripping it with both hands, he approached the sliding doors, which were open. He didn't hear anyone speaking inside, which could mean they were onto him, waiting for his approach.

"It's a wolf!" he heard the guard call, followed by a gunshot.

Using the moment, Joe slipped inside through the open shed doors, keeping to the shadows. He saw an old man talking to a blonde older woman, who turned at the sound of the guard's voice. And seated on a chair, with her hands tied behind her, was Skylar. Beside her stood a thin man with a semiautomatic, which he lifted and pointed toward the wall that faced the birch trees.

They hadn't noticed him. Yet.

Using their sudden state of alert at the sound of the gunshot, Joe slipped to the left. But his motion turned the guard's head and he shouted, "That you, Steven?"

Joe aimed at the guard, and just before he could pull the trigger, he felt a pistol barrel butt up against his temple.

"We've got a visitor," Cole Pruitt said. "Move over there, Cash. Into the light."

Holding up his hands before him, Joe swore silently. Now that he had the opportunity to take in his surroundings, he saw the crates stacked everywhere. No telling what was in those, but the half-dozen freezers against the wall were enough to make him curse. He'd found the mother lode.

Chapter Twenty-Six

Joe stepped out of the shadows, arms raised. His pistol was in one hand. He could aim and fire in a second, if required. But he wanted to show that he was not here for violence or aggression. He could get this done by talking. And he stood a better chance of securing Skylar's safety—and not getting shot himself—if he played along.

"Davis!" he called.

The old man turned to him. The blonde woman standing beside him gripped his arm. A friend or lover? She had to be Skylar's mom. The man he recognized as Reginald Marshall from his mug shot aimed his rifle at Joe.

"We need to talk," Joe said, remaining in place. He stood thirty feet from where Skylar sat. Her body was tense, her gaze burning into him. He couldn't read her expression beyond that she was frightened. "Why do you have Skylar tied up? Is that any way to treat your own family?"

"How'd you find us, boy?" The old man held out his arm, staying his cohort with the rifle. He looked to

Skylar. "You got some kind of GPS on you? Didn't you take her phone after she made the call?"

"I did. And I smashed it like you said," the gunner said. "All the frequency blockers on the property should have blocked any signals."

"It doesn't matter how I found this place," Joe said. "I figure you wanted to talk to me. Here I am. What do you want to say?"

"You got the message. You do as you're told and Skylar goes free."

"And if I don't?"

Malcolm stepped up to stand beside Skylar. "I figure you won't want any harm to come to your lady."

"I just want to take Skylar out of here, safe and unharmed. Will you let me do that?"

"Then what about us?" Davis asked. He cast his glance around. "You going to call in the cavalry?"

Backup should be on the way. But Joe hadn't received confirmation from Dispatch on that; nor did he have service while out in the woods.

"Poaching's not even a felony," Joe offered, trying to appeal to the man's sense of self-preservation. "You'll get a slap on the wrist."

Davis crossed his arms high over his chest and eyed him with that "you can't bullshit me" look. "Poaching is the least of my worries, boy."

Joe nodded. It was hard to dispute that fact. Malcolm had to know that the murder charge he intended to bring against Reginald Marshall was the elephant in the room.

"Now, I know you're an officer, and surrendering your weapon is not something that comes easily to you, but take in the scenario," Davis said. "You're outnumbered. Set down your gun, boy, nice and easy."

To keep Skylar safe, there seemed no other option. Joe nodded and crouched slowly, finally setting his gun on the hay-littered concrete floor. He eyed Skylar. She closed her eyes.

"Kick it over here," Malcolm said.

The last thing he wanted to do was disarm himself, but if Joe could keep them talking until Kofax arrived, he'd be fine. A gentle kick sent the gun across the hay. It stopped three feet away from Davis's boots.

"What the hell?" Cole Pruitt wandered into Joe's peripheral vision. "You fell faster than I expected, Nature Boy."

He'd told Cole how that moniker annoyed him.

"Someone has to look out for Skylar," Joe said, before he could caution himself against making the snide remark.

"And you're doing such a fine job at it," Cole volleyed. "Does it look like you have the upper hand, buddy?"

"I don't want any trouble, Cole. You talk to Mr. Davis and let him know that Skylar has nothing to do with any of this. She needs to walk out of here right now. I'll stay behind. We can talk about this then."

Cole chuckled. "Skylar will come around. Won't you, Sky?" He bent and winked at Skylar, who sneered at him.

"What are we going to do with them?" Reginald Marshall asked. Had he shot at Skylar from across the lake? "Where there's one cop, there's others not far behind."

Cole stepped up to Joe. "Did you call for backup?"

"Didn't have a chance, or cell service," he said. "Found this place by tracking through the forest."

"What?" Cole exchanged glances with Malcolm, then turned an annoyed sneer back on Joe. "I don't believe you. It's a good two- or three-mile trek from Skylar's place. Only one access road here, too, thanks to Skylar hoarding her land and not letting Malcolm pay her a handsome price for a small portion. Someone would have seen you drive up."

"Did you see my car on the road?" Joe asked.

"No." Cole flicked another look over his shoulder to the Davis elder. "We have to get rid of them. Both of them."

The woman stepped up, but Malcolm grabbed her by the wrist. "You said no one would get hurt," she said.

Joe squeezed his fingers into fists. "Murder is not something you want to add to your rap sheet, Cole. What in hell happened to you?"

Cole turned so swiftly Joe barely had time to register the punch aimed at his face. He dodged and took a hit to the shoulder.

A rifle shot echoed loudly in the building and thundered in Joe's ears. He stopped midpunch at Cole, and the first place he looked was the chair where Skylar sat. Tears ran down her cheeks. No one had been shot. Whoever had fired must have done so aiming out the open doorway. But he took the warning and again put up his hands.

This time, he saw the punch coming and had no choice but to let it happen. Cole's fist skimmed his jaw, and Joe twisted at the hip to follow through and take some of the brute power off the contact point. It was a wimpy punch that barely set Joe back a step, but he winced to make it look good.

"Walk away right now," Joe said. "Malcolm's already looking at murder charges. You don't want to be involved with that."

"I do believe you're right," Davis finally said. "This has gotten messy. No thanks to you, Pruitt." He nodded to the gunman. "Reggie, give him your rifle. He'll take care of matters."

"This is my gun," Reggie argued.

"The same gun you used to shoot at Skylar from across the lake?" Joe challenged.

Reggie lifted the gun and aimed it at Joe's head. "Not even close. That one was a real sniper rifle, but this one will serve its purpose—"

"Reggie!" Malcolm admonished. "You've said enough."

Enough for Joe to know he was the guilty party.

"Cole." Malcolm grabbed the gun from Reggie and handed it toward Cole.

"Oh man, I don't want to…" Cole lifted his chin, then nodded. "Fine. Give me that gun. But you'll have to secure Cash's hands behind his back for me if I have to walk them out to the woods."

Davis nodded and his sidekick strode off, probably in search of rope to bind Joe's hands. Which was never going to happen if he wanted to walk out of here alive, and with Skylar at his side.

SKYLAR COULD NOT look Joe in the eyes. She'd glanced at him when Reggie had threatened him with the rifle, but seeing his stoic determination to help her cut into her heart. He was brave and strong, and she wasn't sure what she had done to deserve his kindness. Now he stood at gunpoint while some idiot looked for rope to tie him up—because he planned to kill him. And her.

To top it off, her mother was not arguing strongly for her release. Devastation struggled to reduce Skylar to a sobbing heap, but she had to stay sharp. And hope Joe had a plan.

The old man untied her at the ankles and shoved her shoulder. "Stand up. Cole will take care of you."

"Your brother never said a bad word about you," she said to her uncle. "Even knowing what you were involved in, he was always kind when talking about his family."

"My brother was a fool."

"Did you really murder someone?" Dorothy asked. The tremble in her voice wasn't false, as her proclaimed love for Skylar had been.

Malcolm sucked in his lower lip. "What someone would that be?"

"You know, that old Indian—" Reggie started.

"Reggie! You've got the widest mouth in the county. Now just keep back. My hands are blood-free." Malcolm shoved Skylar, and she stepped toward where Joe stood. "You should have never trusted a cop, Skylar. He brought you down."

"If standing on the right side of the law is down,"

she said to Malcolm, "then I'll join Joseph Cash here on the down side."

She stepped up beside Joe. Feeling his warmth against her shoulder granted her a moment of relief, until she saw Cole wander over with a length of rope.

"Get them out of here." Malcolm turned and walked toward the freezers. He must be unwilling to witness the bloodshed, surely. His hands would never be clean.

Skylar felt Joe's hand clasp hers and squeeze. A teardrop slipped down her cheek. It wouldn't end this way, would it?

"I got you," he said in a low tone.

She wanted to believe that, but their immediate futures looked bleak.

"Turn around," Cole ordered Joe.

When Joe turned and slowly moved his hands behind his back, he looked at Skylar—yet his attention was diverted to the shed doors. Joe gaped, then grinned. And then he winked at Skylar.

She didn't know what was up. Suddenly a wolf's growl sounded. Joe used Cole's sudden distraction to lunge forward and shove Skylar to the side, wrapping an arm about her waist and tugging her out of the way.

Stella soared through the shed doorway and leaped, landing on Cole's chest.

Chapter Twenty-Seven

"Stay low and out of sight," Joe said to Skylar. She nodded, then shuffled over to a crate and knelt.

Joe turned just in time to see the butt of a rifle coming toward him. He kicked high, connecting his foot with Reggie's bicep. The hit was hard and direct. The man yelped in pain, dropping his rifle. Joe spun and landed another kick to the man's gut, and then a successive hit to his thigh, bringing him down, wincing and swearing.

Joe tossed the rifle to Skylar, which she caught and cocked. "Keep an eye on him."

Stella had her maw locked on Cole's bicep, but suddenly the wolf yelped and rolled off the man. A high-pitched whine indicated she'd been injured. Joe hadn't heard a gunshot, so that was one thing to be thankful for.

He charged toward Cole. His former best friend saw him coming, tossed his weapon aside and met Joe's approach with a high kick. "You sic your dog on me, Cash?"

"You're lucky to still be alive," Joe said. He ducked an oncoming punch and spun to swing up his leg.

Cole, despite being injured and bleeding on the arm, was still fast. He dodged, and Joe landed one foot on the ground. Out the corner of his eye he saw Reggie groan, but he was still on the floor, under Skylar's watch.

"There are better ways to get the girl." Cole delivered a kick to Joe's shin.

Bouncing on his feet to alleviate the pain of that hit, Joe worked Cole back toward the crates. Malcolm was nowhere in sight, but Skylar's mother clung to the chair where Skylar had been seated, watching them with fearful eyes.

"It's not about who lost the girl," Joe said. "It's about an old man who got in the way of another man's greed."

"That Indian guy? I had nothing to do with that. Reggie is Malcolm's hit man."

"Good to know." Joe kicked toward Cole's hip, but just as the man stepped aside, Joe transferred his weight to his swinging foot, landing on the floor and sweeping up a fist that clocked his former friend up under the jaw.

Cole landed on the ground, defeated.

The barrel of a gun connected with the back of Joe's neck.

"You've got some fancy fighting skills," old man Davis said. "But I've got all the power."

Joe slowly put up his hands. In the darkness, he couldn't place Skylar, but hoped she was still safe and armed. "Tell me what's in those freezers, Malcolm."

"Why? You hungry for some steak, boy? Move!" He walked Joe over to the freezer where Skylar's mom now stood. "Open it up, Dorothy," Malcolm demanded.

She did so. And revealed an empty freezer.

"The others, too."

All six of them were empty. So why did Joe feel the chilly air each time she opened another? No reason to have a freezer on unless it was in use, or had been in use recently. They'd moved the evidence. And that truck he'd seen before coming in had been refrigerated.

"Not hungry? I can make sure all your steak dinners are comped no matter where you eat," Malcolm offered. "All you have to do is keep your mouth shut."

"I'm a vegetarian. You had eagle parts in there, Davis. You thought Max Owen was a threat to your business, so you had him killed."

"The old man was a nuisance to my bottom dollar, but I'm not a killer, boy."

"No, but your hired gun lying on the floor over there is. He's the same one who left a gift for me on my front step, isn't he?"

Stella barked. Joe turned to find Cole's gun was aimed at the wolf.

"Don't you dare," Joe growled.

Cole's chuckle was followed by a spit of blood to the side. He cocked the rifle. Joe knew the wolf's fate was sealed.

But instead of Cole firing, another gun sounded from behind them both. Davis swore and the gun at Joe's head wobbled. Joe reacted, grabbing the old man's rifle.

Stella yelped and scampered out of the shed.

Joe twisted his gaze to find Skylar standing with her aim now on Cole, who bled from the thigh.

"You shot your fiancé!" Dorothy Davis screamed.

"Stay out of this, Dorothy," Malcolm said. "You've

served no good to nobody since you suggested this cockamamie plan to get the cop on our side."

"Just a flesh wound," Joe offered. "And she's not his fiancé." To Skylar he said, "Keep your aim on Cole while I cuff Malcolm, will you?"

Joe ordered Dorothy to step back, then cuffed Malcolm Davis. When he was finished he walked over to Reggie and punched him. He didn't have another set of cuffs on him, so it was the best way to detain him for now.

After picking up Cole's rifle, Joe pulled Skylar into his embrace. Keeping one eye on the fallen men in the building, he took a few moments to hug the woman.

"Stella saved us," Skylar said.

"That she did."

"Cole would have killed her." She turned to Cole. "You bastard!"

"She would have bitten my face," Cole growled. "I didn't want to hurt you, Skylar. I never would have."

"Tell it to the judge."

The sound of an approaching vehicle crunching across the drive was accompanied by the red flash of police lights on the shed interior.

"The cavalry is here," Joe said.

THREE PATROL CARS parked in the trucking lot, their flashers glowing in the night. Skylar stood back near a wall, arms crossed over her chest, and observed as Joe directed the officers to gather up Malcolm and his men. Calls were put in for more officers and a forensic team.

Joe sent a call to dispatch to stop a refrigerated truck

on County Road 7. Within ten minutes the call came in that the vehicle had been apprehended. A stunning number of eagle carcasses were inside in cold storage.

As Malcolm was led out past Skylar, he sneered at her, then smiled. "This isn't finished," he said.

The hollowness in her gut rose to her throat. No, she imagined it was not. Would the sheriff's department have the guts to convict the man who had bribed some of their own? She certainly prayed for that. But a conviction could destroy Davis Trucking, bringing it all down like the house of cards it was. Skylar could only be thankful Malcolm didn't have a family who would suffer because of their father's dirty dealings.

On the other hand, she hadn't been aware of her mother's involvement with the man. Dorothy had suggested they kidnap Skylar to get Joe on Malcolm's side? Whatever was going on, Dorothy would get what she deserved.

Stella had hightailed it out of there before the first officer had arrived. Skylar had seen she was limping on her front leg, but she'd been determined to escape a scene where so many humans were around. Likely she was in the woods, not far off, licking her wounds. And hopefully those wounds would easily heal.

Dorothy stopped before her, wrists handcuffed behind her back. "I didn't do anything but love the wrong brother."

Skylar winced. "You didn't deserve Merlin Davis."

Her mom bowed her head. "I'm sorry, Skylar."

She didn't know what to say. Dorothy had been in

love with Malcolm? She'd face her with all the questions when the time felt right. Now was not that time.

Rubbing her wrists where the rope had burned, Skylar watched with awe and relief as Joe stood, hands at his hips, observing the operation. He had it under control. Had been willing to sacrifice himself for her release. He'd rescued her.

And maybe she had been waiting for that rescue for a while. Years even. She needed that man in her life. She wanted him around her all the time.

And he was waiting for her to give him the signal.

At that moment, Joe turned, his eyes seeking hers even as officers walked between them, moving things about. A steady calmness lived in his gaze. He had her. Heart and soul.

When he winked, Skylar released the pent-up anxiety and felt a tear pool at the corner of her eye. She flashed a smile his way and nodded. They were good. And she was going home with him tonight.

Epilogue

A week later...

Malcolm Davis was arrested for kidnapping, assault, and poaching endangered species. He posted bail within four hours, but he let Dorothy sit in jail until the next day. She had been charged with collusion to sell animal parts. Apparently, she'd called Skylar after her release, but had left only voice mails.

Skylar had not listened to those messages, erasing them as soon as she'd seen the unknown number on her phone. Her heart wasn't ready for the talk she needed to have with her mother. Was it even necessary? She'd left her life so long ago. Skylar had moved on. She needed time to think and sort out whether reconciling with her mom would improve her life or just make it miserable.

There was the issue that she owned half of Skylar's land, so she would have to speak to her sooner rather than later. Suspicions were that Dorothy would not give up her half once she learned about it. Especially not if she was now seeing Malcolm. It would be his way to nab what he wanted.

Skylar would face that challenge. Somehow.

Cole Pruitt, charged with poaching, had paid a fine of eight thousand dollars and was allowed to enter rehab in a Minneapolis facility. He'd apologized to Joe but not to Skylar. Joe felt that had been backward, but Skylar had insisted he let it drop. She was just thankful the man was seeking help for his alcohol problem. One that had likely occurred because of the stresses of working for Malcolm Davis.

Reginald Marshall had been charged with murder. His fingerprints had been lifted from the newspaper that had covered the eagle left on Joe's front stoop. The same lead-tainted strychnine that had been on that eagle had also been on the one that had ended Max Owen's life. As well, he owned a Lapua rifle, and the ballistics forensic team had been able to match it to the bullets that Joe had collected from Skylar's yard. Currently sitting in jail, he awaited a trial.

Joe stood beside Stella under the shade of the paper birch trees that shivered in the wind. The two of them watched Skylar take measurements for the shelter building she planned to put up on the west side of her house. Now, more than ever, she was determined to raise the money to build the place. After Joe had suggested she try a Kickstarter program, Skylar had said she'd consider it. He knew she didn't like to take charity. That fierce, independent streak ran red in her veins. And he had offered to invest, which she'd also refused.

She would find a way to build her dreams. And that she'd allow him to stand beside her while it happened? There was nothing better in this world for him to do.

"Where's the goat section going?" Joe asked.

Skylar made a few leaps toward the center of the area she'd marked out. "Right here. And over there I want a nursery that I can keep stocked with an incubator. I've got big plans, Joe."

"That you do. You'll make it. I know you will."

"I love that you have such faith in me. But there's still the issue of my mother owning half the land. You know Malcolm will pounce as soon as we reveal that to her."

"You talk to the lawyer about loopholes in the will? Maybe she forfeited rights by disappearing for so long."

Skylar shrugged. "Maybe. My lawyer is looking into it. It all depends on probate."

"It's something to explore. But whatever happens, I'm here for you."

"After all we've been through, you still give me the benefit of the doubt. Why do you do that, Joseph Cash?"

He pulled her into a hug and bowed to kiss her head. "Because I'm in love with you. And whatever makes you smile makes me smile, too."

"You know, you telling me you love me should freak me out."

"So does it?"

"Nope. I kind of like it. Might even get used to it."

"I mean it."

"I know you do." She pushed up on her tiptoes and kissed him. "Here's to a bright future."

"No more burned wedding dresses?"

"Not in the foreseeable future." She laughed. "Next time I decide to say 'I do,' it'll be because my heart wants me to, not because my brain thinks it needs something stupid."

"This heart is not stupid," he said, laying his palm over her breast where he could feel her heartbeats.

"No, it's not." She kissed him again, and said, "I'm falling in love with you, wolf whisperer. Or maybe I've loved you for a long time and have finally realized it."

"I'll take it either way."

She kissed him, then tapped the eagle talon at his throat. "I know it doesn't heal your heart, but did learning about Max's death answer some questions for you?"

"It did. I will mourn the man. He was a mentor. I think he knows that I found the truth for him. Wherever he is right now, he's teaching and guiding."

"You're following in your mentor's footsteps."

"I hope so. This arrest didn't take out a key player like I had hoped, but it has called attention to the eagle poaching. Got a couple interviews with local news stations under my belt. I'm not going to stop talking about it until the laws and fines are so harsh that poachers will think twice before taking another animal life. I'm going to talk at a school next week about it."

"Really? You should bring along Stella. She'd make a great mascot for your cause."

"Yeah?" Joe patted his thigh and Stella tilted her head to look up at the twosome. "You cool with that, Stella?"

Stella yipped and then pounced playfully beside him, wagging her tail.

"I think she's challenging me to a race," Joe said.

"Come on!" He grabbed Skylar's hand and the two of them raced to the house, with Stella loping along behind them.

* * * * *

We hope you enjoyed Joe's story.
If you are interested in his brother Jason's story
please look for Storm Warning
at your favorite online retailer.

COMING NEXT MONTH FROM

◆ HARLEQUIN®

INTRIGUE

Available November 19, 2019

#1893 SAFETY BREACH
Longview Ridge Ranch • by Delores Fossen
Former profiler Gemma Hanson is in witness protection, but she's still haunted by memories of the serial killer who tried to kill her last year. Her concerns skyrocket when Sheriff Kellan Slater tells her the murderer has learned her location and is coming to finish what he started.

#1894 UNDERCOVER ACCOMPLICE
Red, White and Built: Delta Force Deliverance
by Carol Ericson
When Delta Force soldier Hunter Mancini learns the group that kidnapped CIA operative Sue Chandler is now framing his team leader, he asks for her help. But could she be hiding something that would clear his boss?

#1895 AMBUSHED AT CHRISTMAS
Rushing Creek Crime Spree • by Barb Han
After a jogger resembling Detective Leah Cordon is murdered, rancher Deacon Kent approaches her, believing the attack is related to recent cattle mutilations. Can they find the killer before he corners Leah?

#1896 DANGEROUS CONDITIONS
Protectors at Heart • by Jenna Kernan
Former soldier Logan Lynch's first investigation as the constable of a small town leads him to microbiologist Paige Morris, whose boss was killed. Yet as they search for the murderer, Paige is forced to reveal a secret that shows the stakes couldn't be higher.

#1897 RULES IN DEFIANCE
Blackhawk Security • by Nichole Severn
Blackhawk Security investigator Elliot Dunham never expected his neighbor to show up bruised and covered in blood in the middle of the night. To protect Waylynn Hargraves, Elliot must defy the rules he's set for himself, because he knows he's all that stands between her and certain death.

#1898 HIDDEN TRUTH
Stealth • by Danica Winters
When undercover CIA agent Trevor Martin meets Sabrina Parker, the housekeeper at the ranch where he's lying low, he doesn't know she's an undercover FBI agent. After a murder on the property, the operatives must work together, but can they discover their hidden connection before it's too late?

YOU CAN FIND MORE INFORMATION ON UPCOMING HARLEQUIN® TITLES, FREE EXCERPTS AND MORE AT WWW.HARLEQUIN.COM.

HICNM1119

Get 4 FREE REWARDS!

We'll send you 2 FREE Books
plus 2 FREE Mystery Gifts.

Harlequin Intrigue® books feature heroes and heroines that confront and survive danger while finding themselves irresistibly drawn to one another.

FREE
Value Over
$20

"Why did you say you owed me?" she asked.

The question came out of the blue and threw him, so much so that he gulped down too much coffee and nearly choked. Hardly the reaction for a tough-nosed cop. But his reaction to her hadn't exactly been all badge, either.

Kellan lifted his shoulder and wanted to kick himself for ever bringing it up in the first place. Bad timing, he thought, and wondered if there would ever be a good time for him to grovel.

"I didn't stop Eric from shooting you that night." He said that fast. Not a drop of sugarcoating. "You, my father and Dusty. I'm sorry for that."

Her silence and the shimmering look in her eyes made him stupid, and that was the only excuse he could come up with for why he kept talking.

"It's easier for me to toss some of the blame at you for not ID'ing a killer sooner," he added. And he still did blame her, in part, for that. "But it was my job to stop him before he killed two people and injured another while he was right under my nose."

The silence just kept on going. So much so that Kellan turned, ready to go back to his desk so that he wouldn't continue to prattle on. Gemma stopped him by putting her hand on his arm. It was like a trigger that sent his gaze searching for hers. Wasn't hard to find when she stood and met him eye to eye.

"It was easier for me to toss some of the blame at you, too." She made another of those sighs. "But there was no stopping Eric that night. The stopping should have happened prior to that. I should have seen the signs." When he started to speak, Gemma lifted her hand to silence him. "And please don't tell me that it's all right, that I'm not at fault. I don't think I could take that right now."

Unfortunately, Kellan understood just what she meant. They were both still hurting, and a mutual sympathyfest was only going to make it harder. They couldn't go back. Couldn't undo. And that left them with only one direction. Looking ahead and putting this son of a bitch in a hole where he belonged.

Don't miss Safety Breach *by Delores Fossen,*
available December 2019 wherever
Harlequin® Intrigue books and ebooks are sold.

Harlequin.com